CU00543265

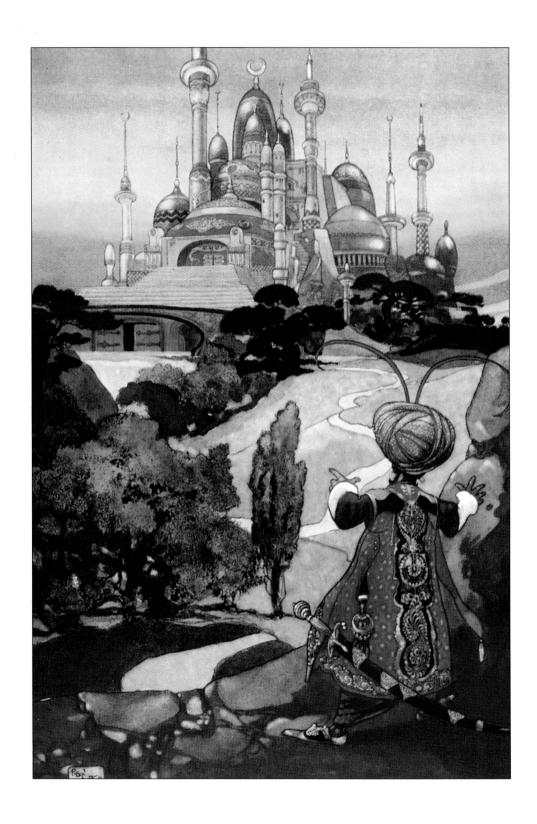

He saw before him a building of black polished marble

René Bull, 1912

Arabian Nights

ILLUSTRATED

Art of Dulac, Folkard, Parrish and Others

Selected and Edited by Jeff A. Menges

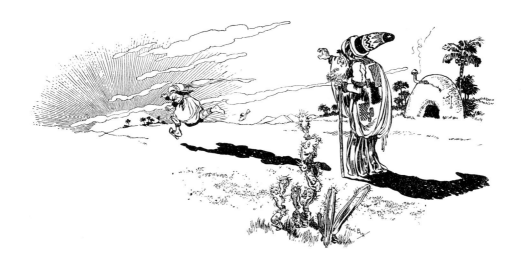

DOVER PUBLICATIONS, INC.

Mineola, New York

Copyright

Copyright © 2008 by Dover Publications, Inc.
Introduction and biographical notes copyright © 2008 by Jeff A. Menges
All rights reserved.

Bibliographical Note

This Dover edition, first published in 2008, is an original compilation of illustrations from the following sources: *The Arabian Nights*, Will and Frances Brundage (Raphael Tuck & Sons, London, Paris, and New York, 1893); *The Arabian Nights Entertainments*, H. J. Ford (Longmans, Green, and Co., London, New York, and Bombay, 1898); *The Arabian Nights' Entertainments*, Thomas B. Dalziel and A. W. Cooper (George Routledge and Sons, Ltd., London, 1902); *The Arabian Nights: Their Best-Known Tales*, Maxfield Parrish (Charles Scribner's Sons, New York, 1909); *The Arabian Nights*, René Bull (Bell and Cockburn, Toronto, 1912); *Stories from the Arabian Nights*, Edmund Dulac (Hodder and Stoughton, London, 1907) and *Sindbad the Sailor & Other Stories from the Arabian Nights*, Edmund Dulac (Hodder and Stoughton, London, 1914); *The Arabian Nights*, Charles Folkard (A. & C. Black, Ltd. London, 1913); *The Story of Prince Ahmed and the Fairy Perie Banou*, Charles Robinson (Gay and Hancock, London, 1913); *The Arabian Nights Entertainments*, Milo Winter (Rand McNally & Company, Chicago and New York, 1914); *The Arabian Nights' Entertainments*, Louis Rhead (Harper & Brothers, New York and London, 1916); and *Aladdin and his Wonderful Lamp: In Rhyme*, Arthur Ransome, Illustrations by Thomas Mackenzie (Nisbet & Co., London, 1920).

NOTE: Caption punctuation varies according to the original source.

Library of Congress Cataloging-in-Publication Data

Arabian nights illustrated : art of Dulac, Folkard, Parrish and others / selected and edited by Jeff A. Menges.
    p. cm.
    ISBN-13: 978-0-486-46522-7
    ISBN-10: 0-486-46522-5
    1. Illustration of books—Great Britain—19th century. 2. Illustration of books—United States—19th century. 3. Illustration of books—Great Britain—20th century. 4. Illustration of books—United States—20th century. 5. Arabian nights—Illlustrations. I. Menges, Jeff A.
  NC978.A67 2008
  741.6'4—dc22

2008006611

Manufactured in the United States of America
Dover Publications, Inc., 31 East 2nd Street, Mineola, N.Y. 11501

FOR COLEMAN

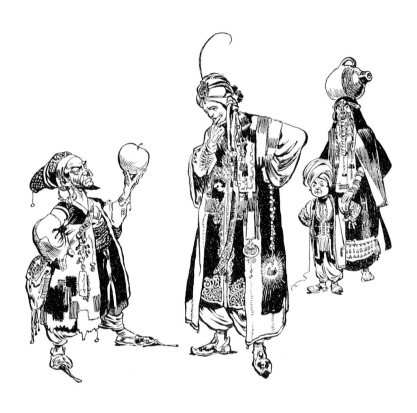

"The Arabian Nights is more generally loved than Shakespeare . . . No human face or voice greets us among [this] crowd of kings and genies, sorcerers and beggarmen. Adventure, on the most naked terms, furnishes forth the entertainment and is found enough."

—Robert Louis Stevenson

Introduction

The mention of the Arabian Nights steers the mind away from mundane matters and everyday surroundings to visions of genies and flying carpets, caverns overflowing with treasure, and the tear-drop-shaped domes of Eastern lands: We immediately are transported to a realm of exotic legend. That journey is the purpose of the tales illustrated in this captivating book, a journey for both the subject of the tale-within-the-tale framework, and for the modern reader.

Storytelling also provides the context for these narratives: an exotic and dangerous setting in which the lovely, ingenious Scheherazade spins out one-thousand-and-one tales for her husband, the Sultan, who is bent on his wife's eventual execution. As long as the Sultan is entertained by the tales—and desires to hear "just one more"—the clever Scheherazade is spared. This strange and wonderful escape to distant magical lands attracted eighteenth- and nineteenth-century European readers to these tales, which still are cherished today.

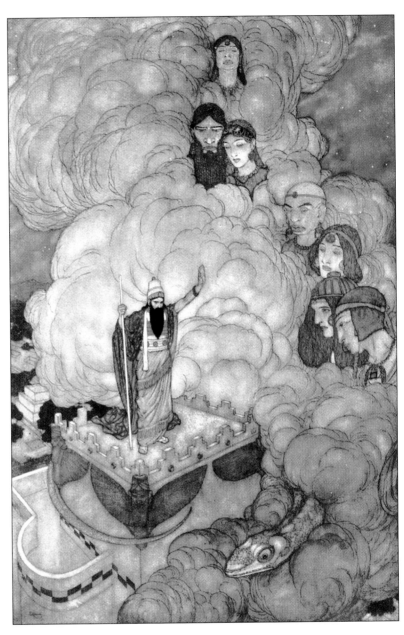

"When having brought into submission all the rest of my race"
Stories from the Arabian Nights, Edmund Dulac, 1907

Set in eighth-century Baghdad, the enchanting stories, and their ingenious framework, have continually captured the imagination of Western readers. The history of this collection of stories has roots that go back centuries; the sources for the material seem to be as numerous as the tales themselves. Professor Antoine Galland translated the bulk of the material we know as the Arabian Nights from Arabic into French in 1704 (the twelve-volume *Les Milles et une Nuits*). Notably, not only did Galland remove much of the poetry from the original—he also excised

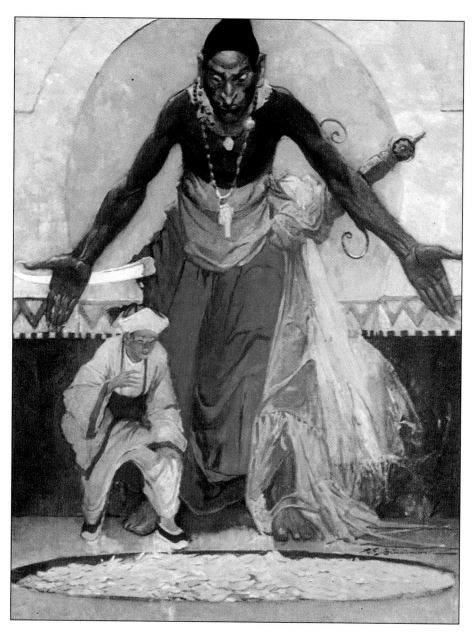

Frontispiece for the 1916 Harper and Brothers edition
The Arabian Nights Entertainments, Frank Schoonover, 1916

segments that he believed to be unsuitable for the European reader. The translation was a tremendous success, as storytelling and fairy tales were major forms of entertainment for all ages, and this previously unknown material, set in a location as fantastic as the narratives, was eagerly received. Galland's tales, and those that would emerge in later translations and interpretations, have provided an alternate canvas for some familiar stories and also have introduced to the Western world tales that seem to have no counterpart in our mythologies.

During the late nineteenth century, a fascination with Eastern culture created a movement in the arts known as Orientalism, reflecting England's strong colonial presence in India, Egypt, and Hong Kong. Global trade was flourishing due to improvements in transportation, and, in the publishing world, beautifully illustrated books could be produced and made available at a cost that placed them, for the first time, in the hands of more than a select few.

The Arabian Nights offers creative possibilities for an illustrator that are nearly unmatched by other works. These are wild and inventive tales, with magic, the supernatural, and many sorts of imaginary beings—all the rich imagery that a visual storyteller could hope for. Sir Richard Burton, who translated a pioneering version of the tales into sixteen volumes in English, said, "The marvelous imaginativeness of the tales produces an insensible brightness of mind and an increase of fancy—power, making one dream that behind them lies the new and the unseen, the strange and the unexpected—in fact, all the glamour of the unknown." What more could an illustrator hope for?

Here, then, is a collection of many of the best visuals to ever accompany these stories, from some of the earliest illustrated printings in the West, to the influence of the Art Deco movement. Edmund Dulac's jewel-like colors, René Bull's confident line work, and Thomas Mackenzie's stylish interpretations are included within, along with many images that have not been reprinted in three-quarters of a century or more. Like Galland's tales, the Arabian Nights offer an embarrassment of riches, one that is best shared.

Jeff A. Menges
January 2008

Artists & Volumes

Frontispiece René Bull, 1912: He saw before him a building of black polished marble
Title page René Bull, 1912: ". . . called to me as loud as he could to return."
Dedication page René Bull: 1912, "Let me see that apple," said the Prince.

The Plates

Opposite: Queen Scheherazade relating the story

Frances Brundage, 1893

Will and Frances Brundage
The Arabian Nights, 1893

In the mid to late nineteenth century, the earliest color works to be printed on a commercial scale were produced through chromolithography. Not a direct reproduction, this technique relied on the interpretation by the lithographer to accurately reproduce the color effects of a painting by adding one color at a time to the image surface. The works from this 1893 edition of *The Arabian Nights* use chromolithography—as does much of the work of Frances Brundage (1854–1937). A prolific and popular American illustrator, she was well known for her postcard and calendar work in the early twentieth century. Children were a particularly strong focus for her, both as an audience and as subject matter. In 1886 Frances married artist William Tyson Brundage (1849–1923), and his name shares the credit on more than one of the plates in this group.

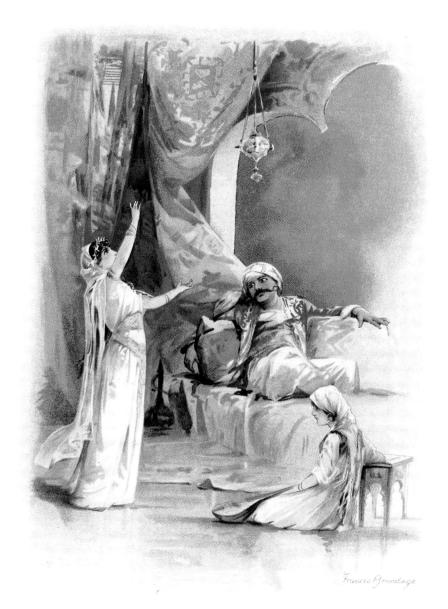

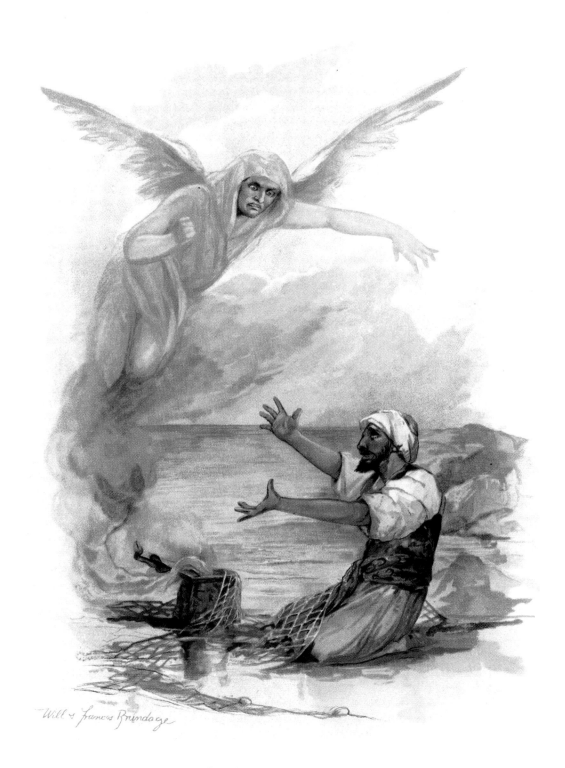

The Fisherman and the Genie

Will and Frances Brundage, 1893

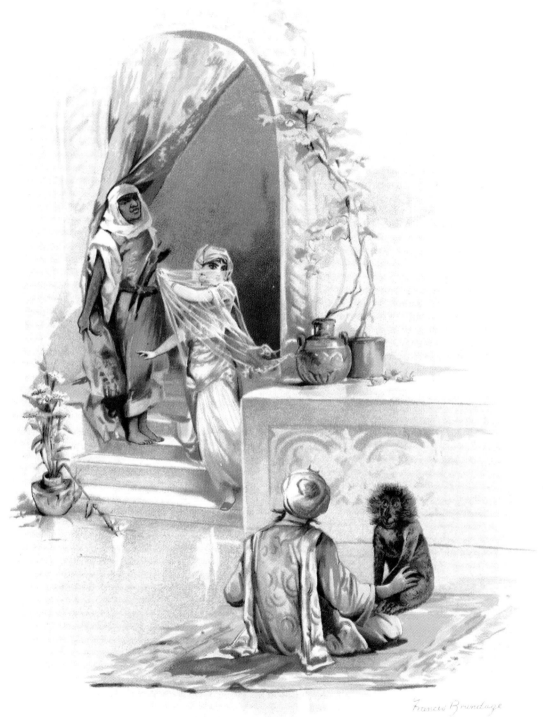

The Queen of Beauty

Frances Brundage, 1893

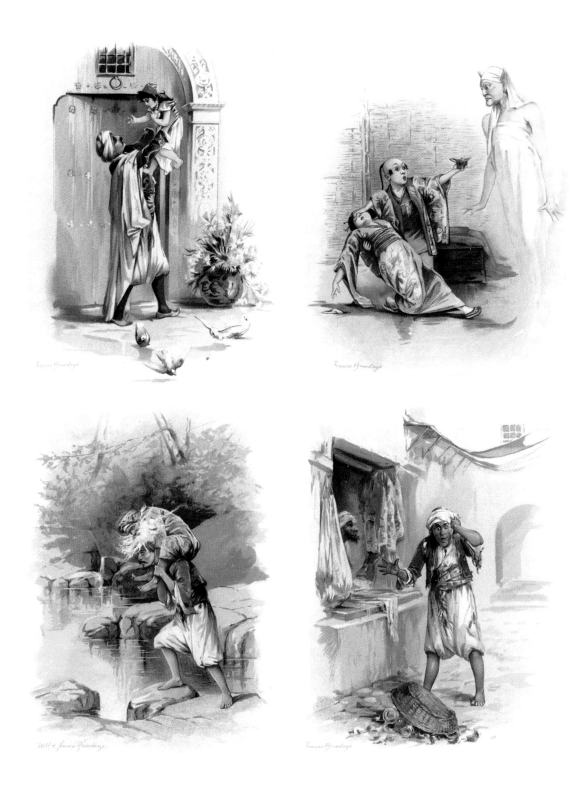

Top left: The Three Apples
Top right: Aladdin and his Wonderful Lamp
Bottom left: The Old Man of the Sea
Bottom right: The Barber's Fifth Brother

Bottom left by Will and Frances Brundage; others by Frances Brundage, 1893

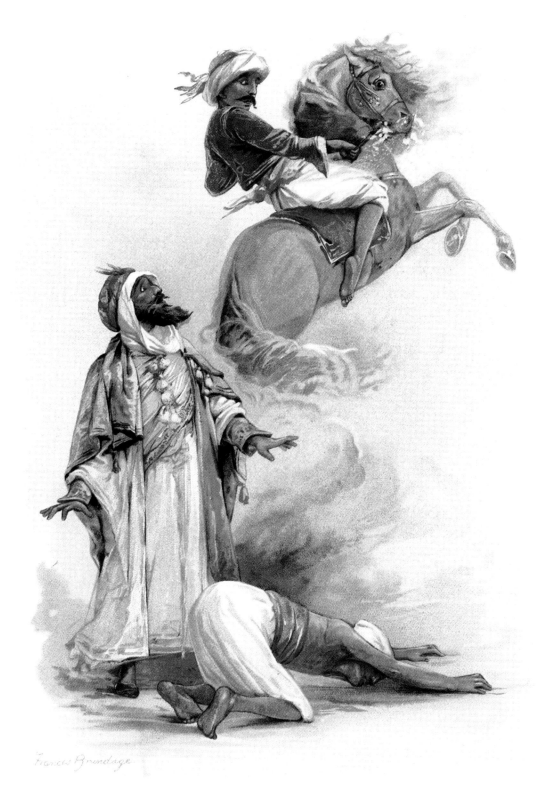

The Enchanted Horse

Frances Brundage, 1893

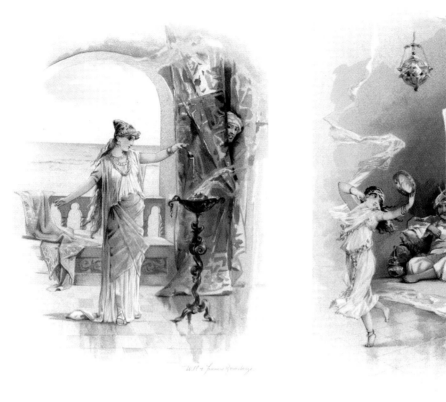

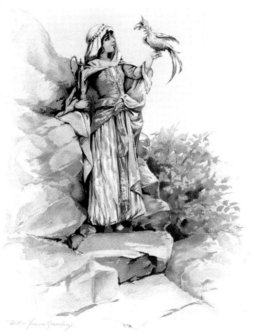

Top left: Princess Gulnare summoning her Relatives
Top right: Morgiana entertaining the Captain
Bottom: The Talking Bird

Top left and bottom by Will and Frances Brundage; top right by Frances Brundage, 1893

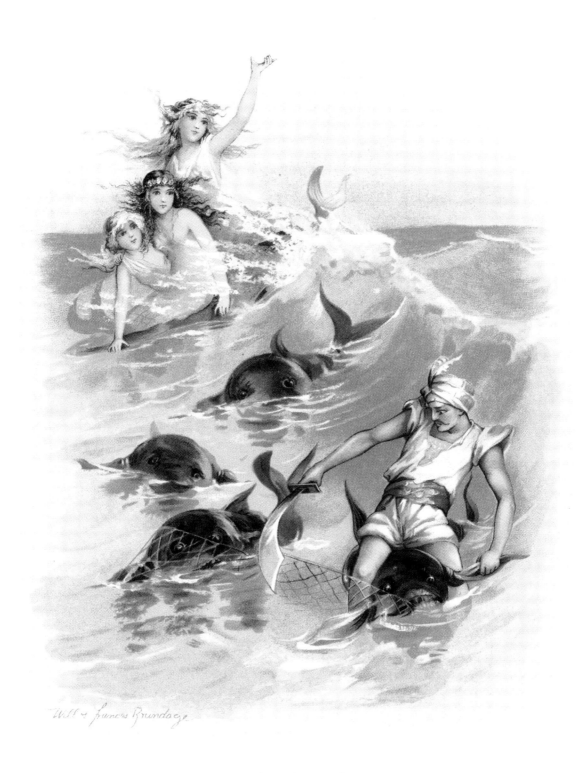

The Arabian Knight

Will and Frances Brundage, 1893

Opposite left: He saw a Genie of monstrous bulk advancing towards him
Opposite right: "The stranger was a sorcerer"

René Bull, 1912

René Bull

THE ARABIAN NIGHTS, 1912

Bull was born in Dublin, Ireland, in 1872. His early artistic career had roots in London and Paris; his training in illustration advanced as he depicted war for numerous conflicts in turn-of-the-century Europe, India, Africa, and the Middle East. Bookwork marked his career from 1905 to just after WWI. His familiarity with Arab customs, due to his years in war coverage, provided Bull with an edge when working on *The Rubáiyát of Omar Khayyám* and *The Arabian Nights.* Among Arabian Nights volumes, Bull's is among those most prized for their illustrations, due to their consistently strong quality. Bull died in 1942.

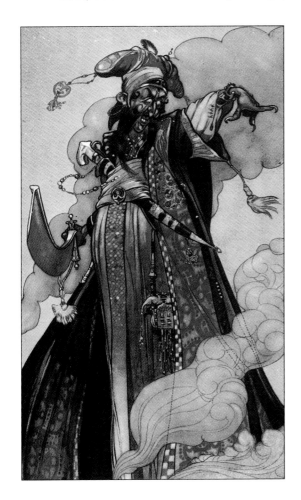

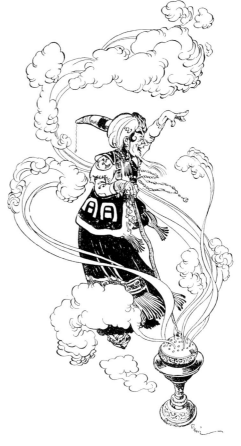

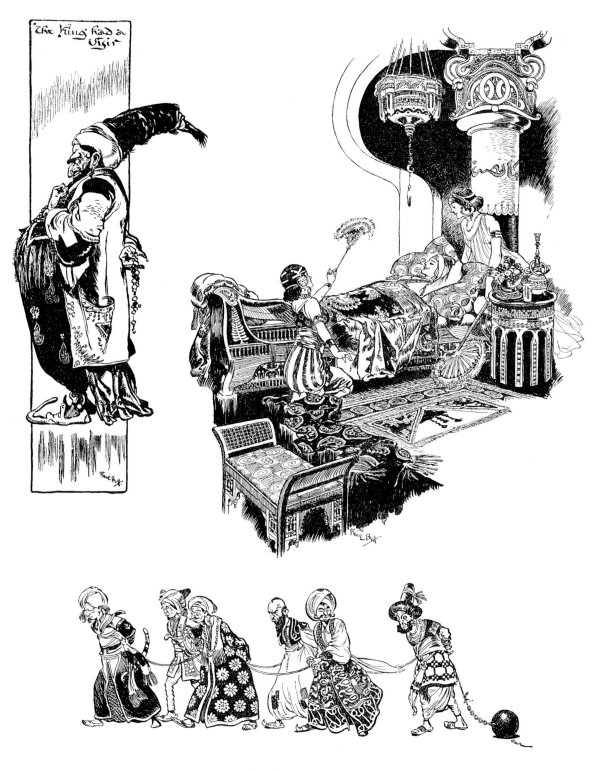

Top left: The King had a Vizir
Top right: "They thought I was asleep, and spoke in whispers."
Bottom: "I and five of my comrades . . ."

René Bull, 1912

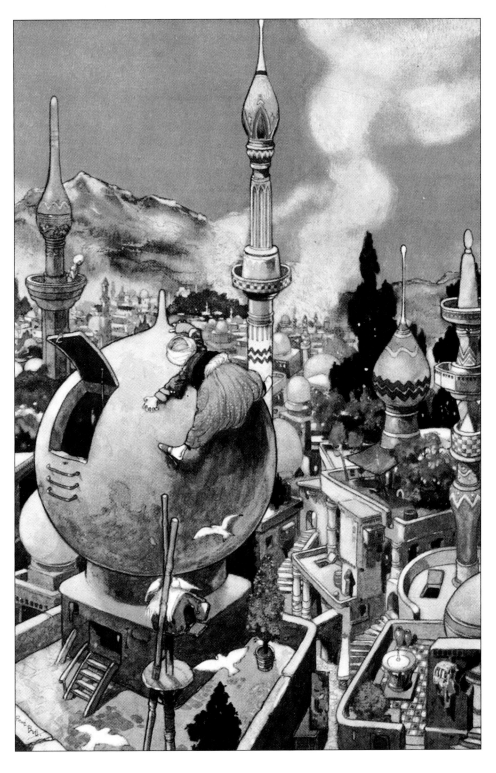

She transported me in a moment from the island to the roof of my own house

René Bull, 1912

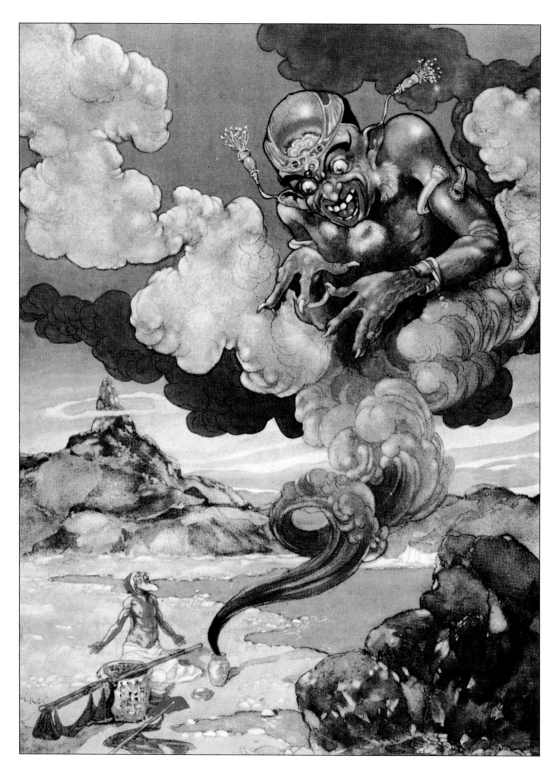

Ah! replied the fisherman, why would you kill me?

René Bull, 1912

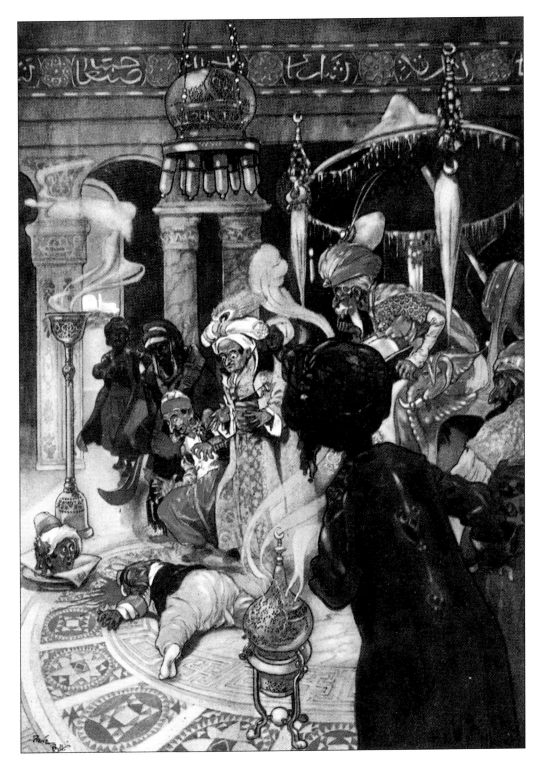

Turn over some more leaves, replied the head

René Bull, 1912

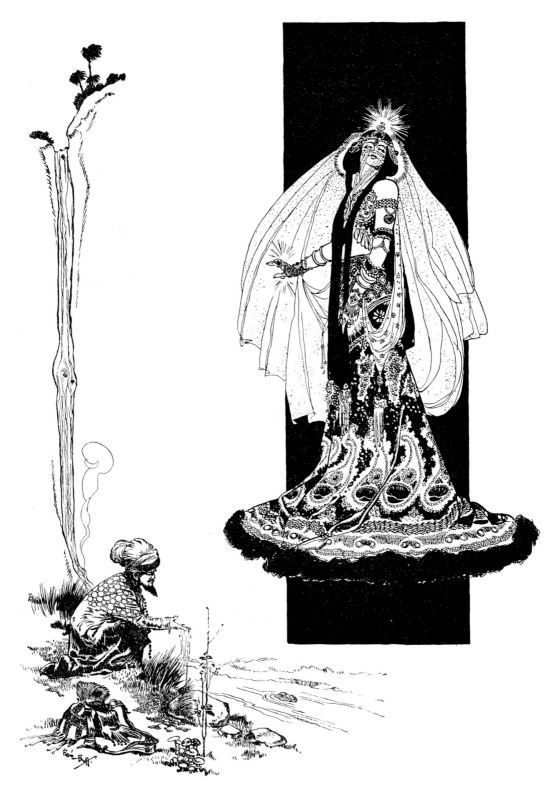

Left: "... he found a fountain of clear water"
Right: "... a female of exceeding beauty"

René Bull, 1912

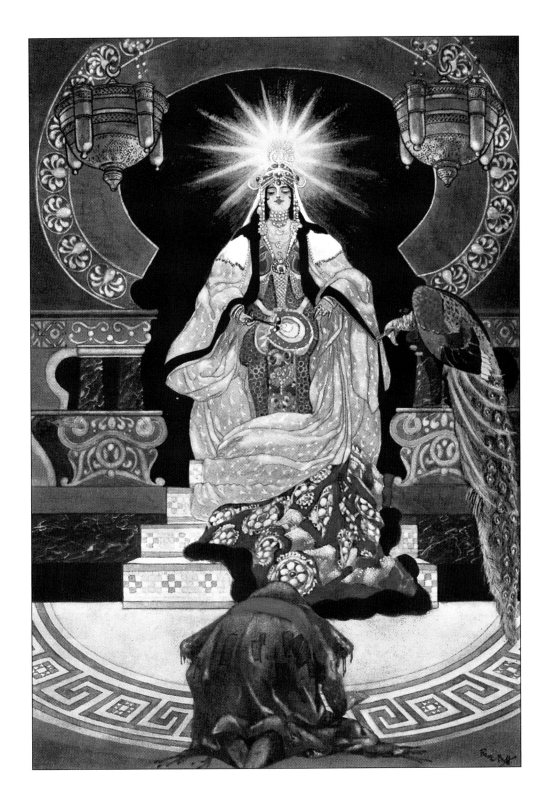

Perie Banou was seated in this hall

René Bull, 1912

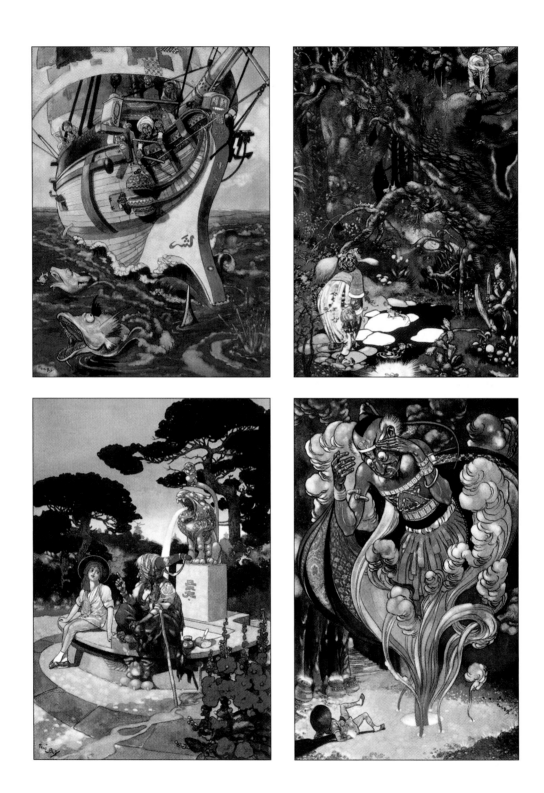

Top left: I saw fishes of a hundred and two hundred cubits long
Top right: He was much alarmed when he saw me
Bottom left: On the brink of a fountain of clear water
Bottom right: A genie of frightful aspect rose

René Bull, 1912

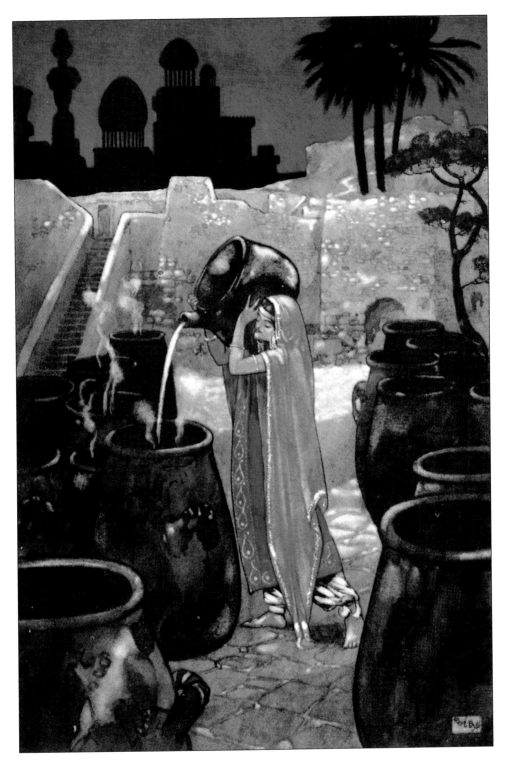

And poured enough into every jar

René Bull, 1912

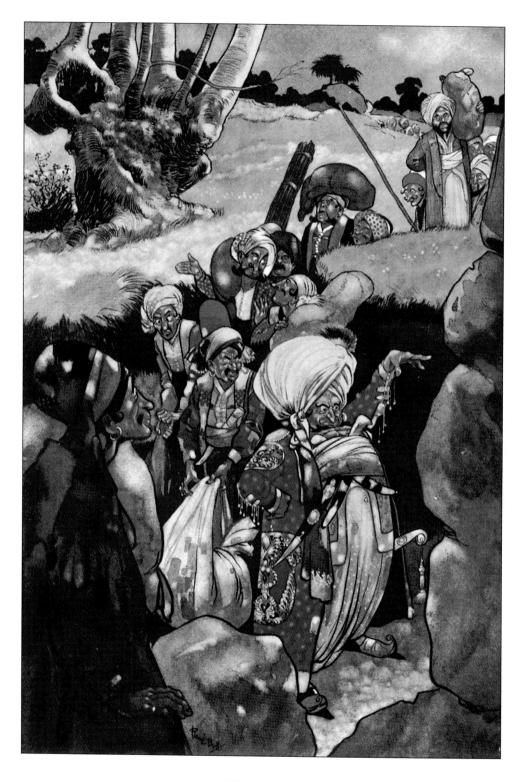

Open Sesame

René Bull, 1912

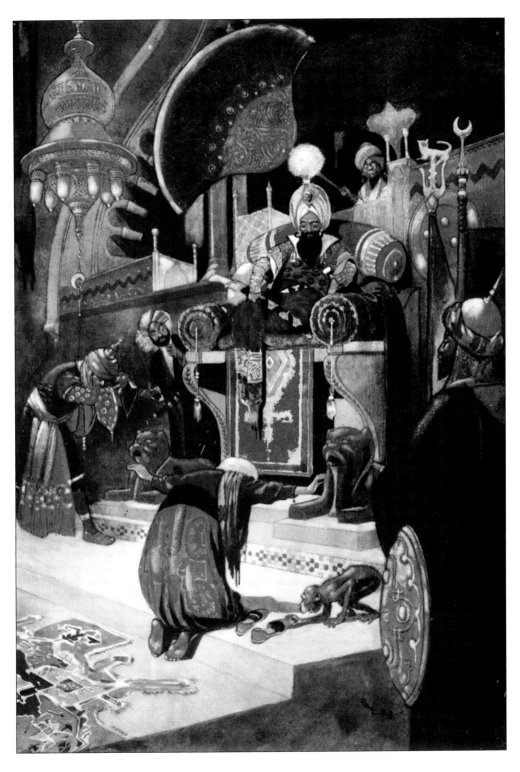

I prostrated myself at his feet

René Bull, 1912

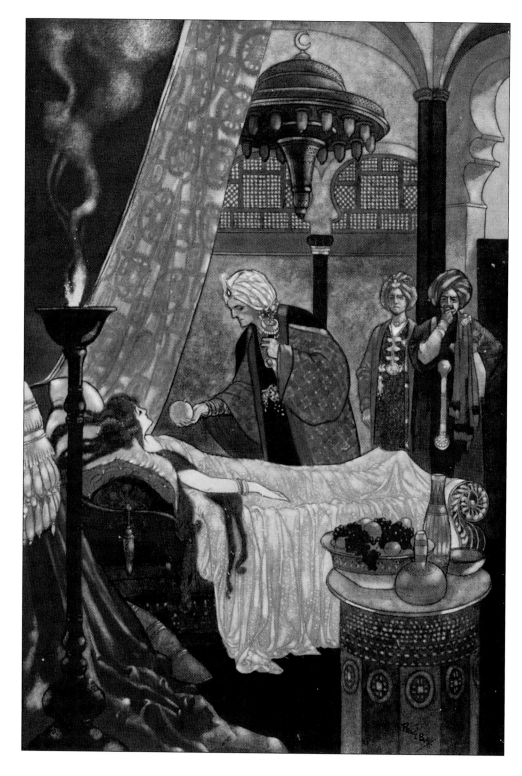

Put the apple to her nostrils

René Bull, 1912

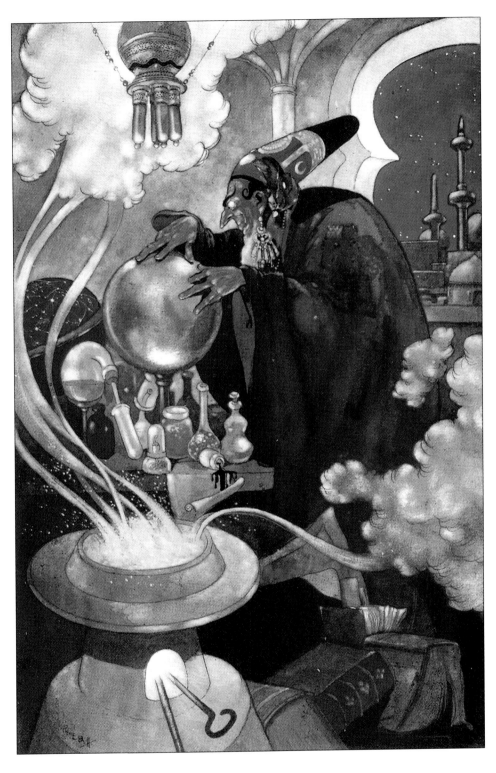

After a long and careful course of magical inquiries

René Bull, 1912

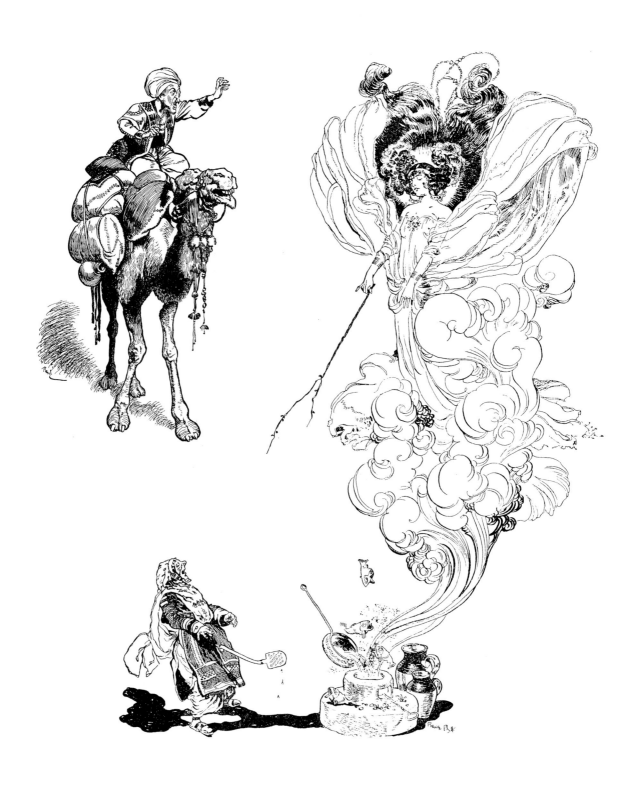

Left: "…I called to him as loud as I could"
Right: "…a young lady of wonderful beauty entered"

René Bull, 1912

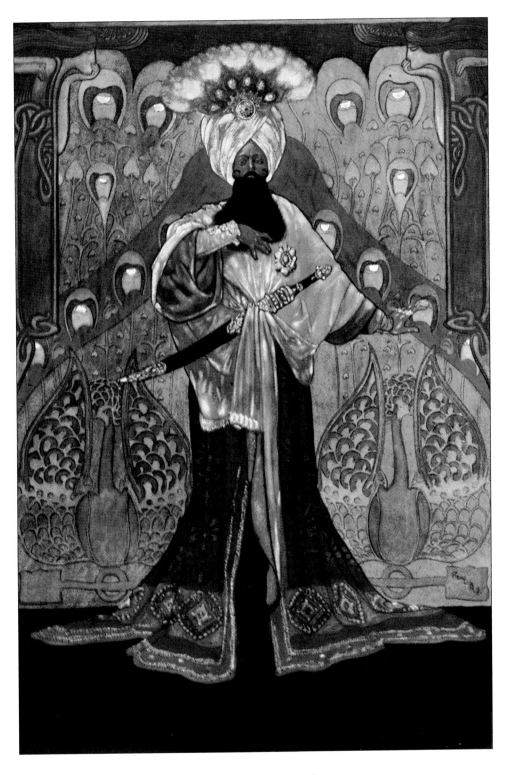

The Caliph Haroun al Raschid

René Bull, 1912

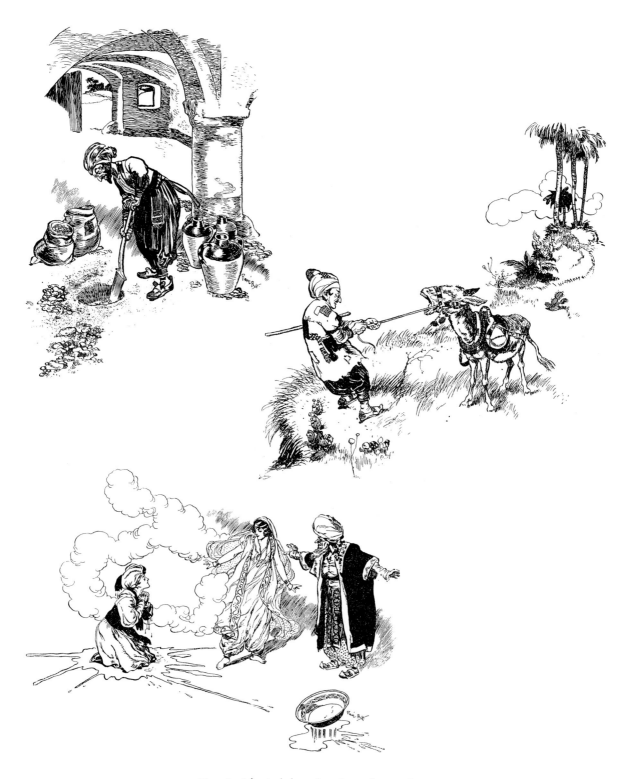

Top: "…I buried the other three thousand"
Center: "…he could scarcely stand when he came back"
Bottom: "…he in an instant recovered his natural form"

René Bull, 1912

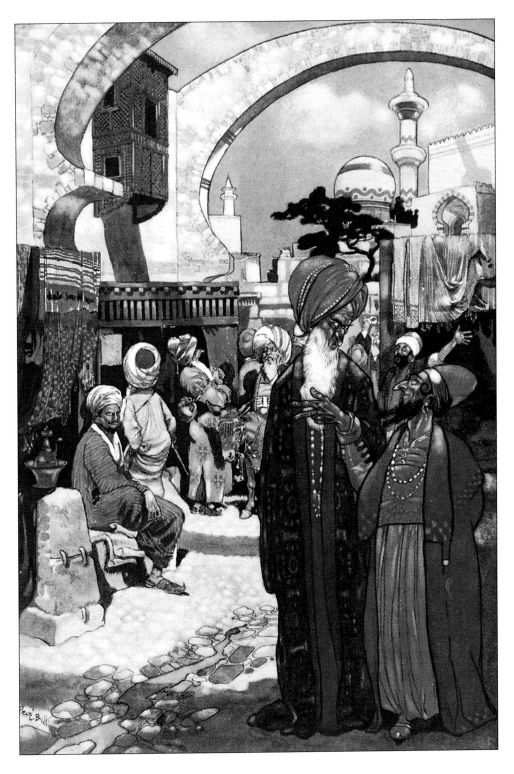

Ali Cogia heard these words

René Bull, 1912

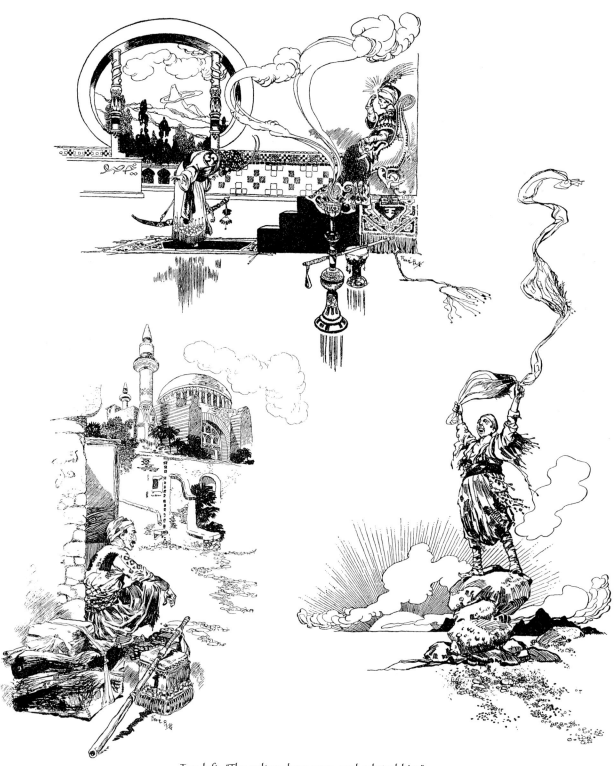

Top left: "The sultan drew near, and saluted him"
Bottom left: "...sat down near a great house to rest"
Bottom right: "I called as loud as I could"

René Bull, 1912

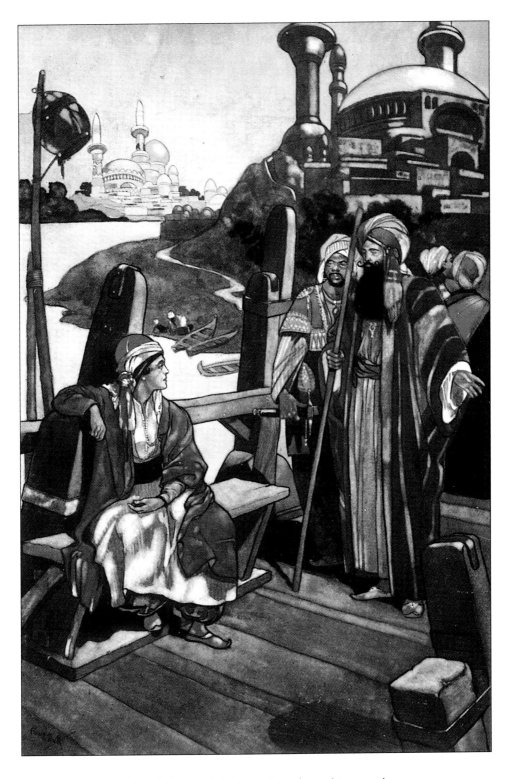

The Caliph attended by one slave chanced to come by

René Bull, 1912

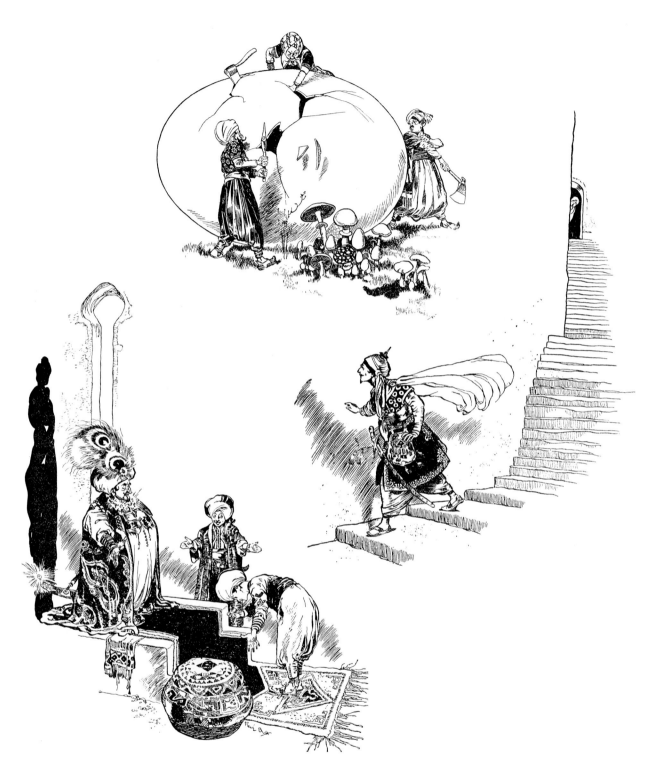

Top: "The merchants…broke the egg with hatchets"
Center: "His grief was so extreme, that he left the court"
Bottom: "I…was presented to the Maha-râjah"

René Bull, 1912

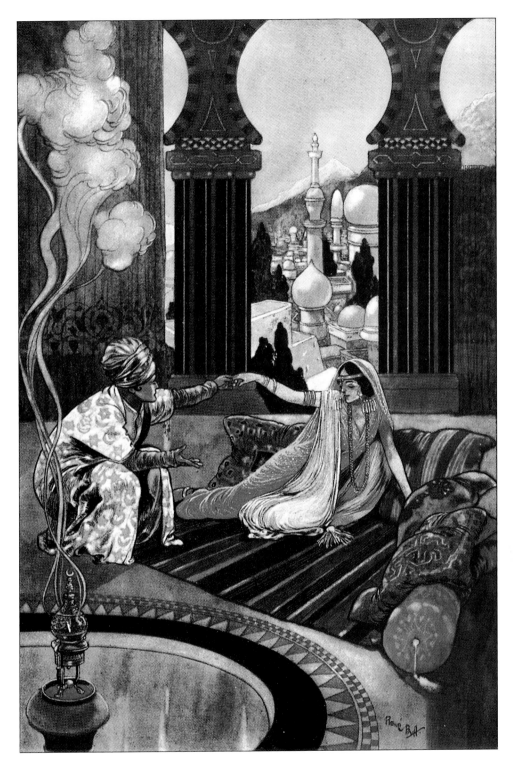

He made her sit down by him

René Bull, 1912

Opposite: The thief

Thomas B. Dalziel, 1902

Dalziel and Cooper

The Arabian Nights Entertainments, 1902

Thomas Dalziel (1823–1906) was one of four brothers who were among the best wood engravers of the mid-Victorian period in England. Engraving onto wood a drawing prepared by an artist was an integral part of the illustration process from the early nineteenth to early twentieth centuries. It required a skilled craftsman who possessed an interpretive eye and an understanding for the material. Dalziel occasionally created his own illustrations, many of which were included in the 1865 edition published by Ward Lock. The color plates published in this volume that accompany Dalziel's cuts are chromolithographs, done after the work of the English artist A. W. Cooper. They are among the earliest color illustrations for these stories.

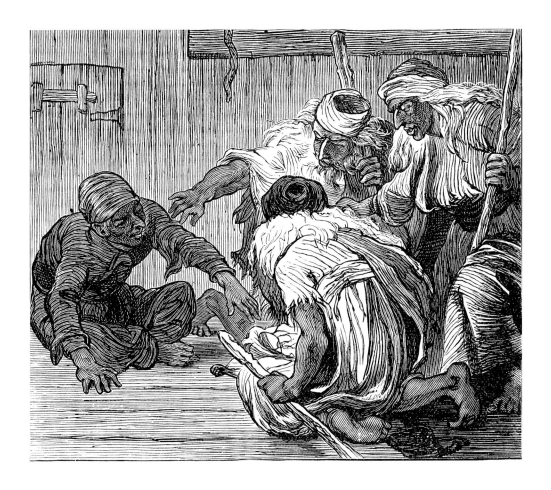

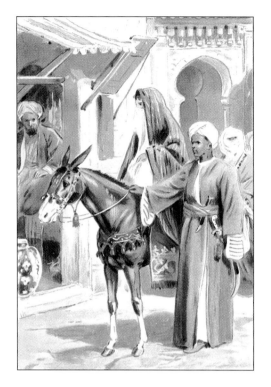 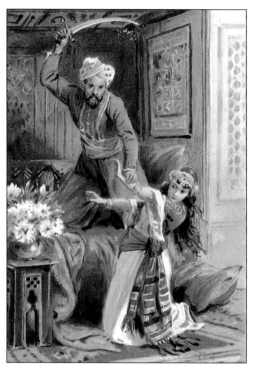

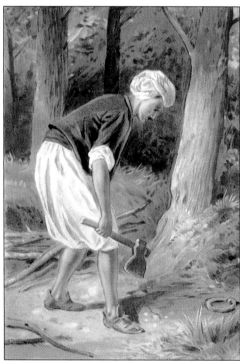 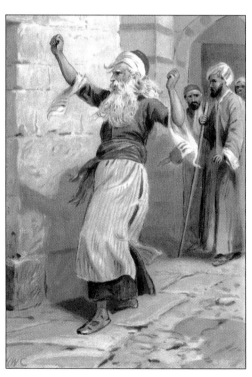

Top left: "... they observed a lady come to the door mounted on a black and white mule ..."

Top right: "Wretched woman," replied the sultan

Bottom left: "In cutting up the root of a tree, I discovered an iron ring ..."

Bottom right: "They knocked furiously at the door of the cadi"

A. W. Cooper, 1902

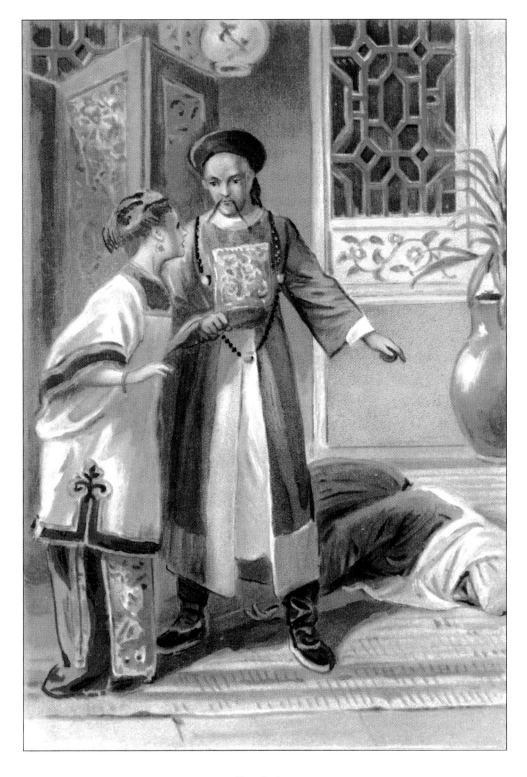

Frontispiece

A. W. Cooper, 1902

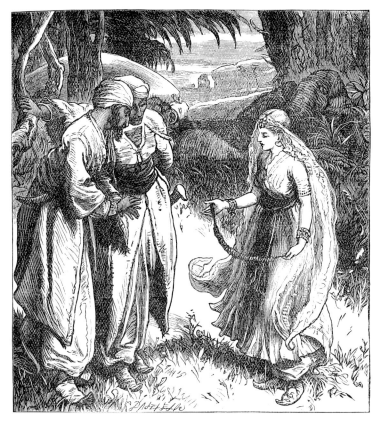

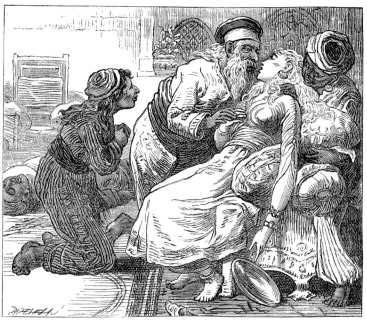

Top: The Lady and the princes
Bottom: Death of the princess

Thomas B. Dalziel, 1902

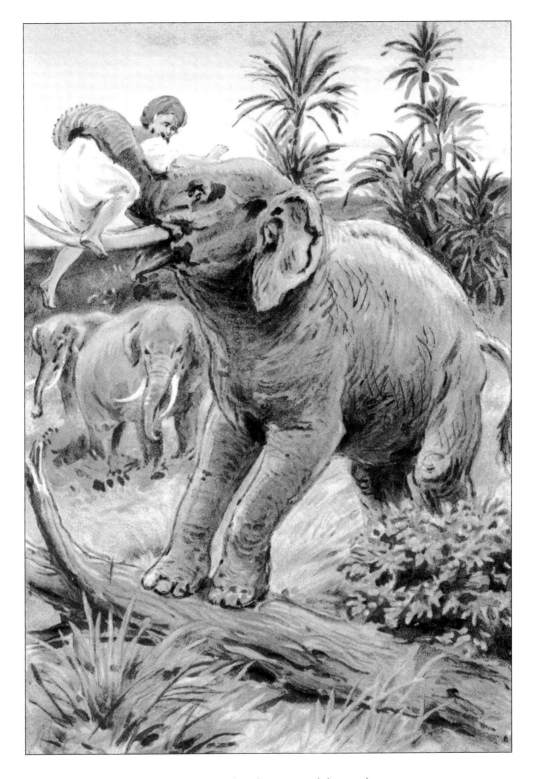

".. . but the animal took me up with his trunk ..."

A. W. Cooper, 1902

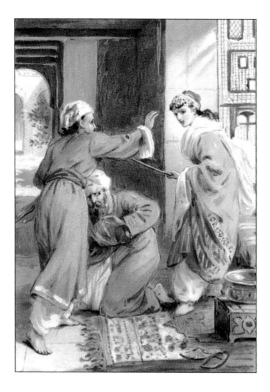
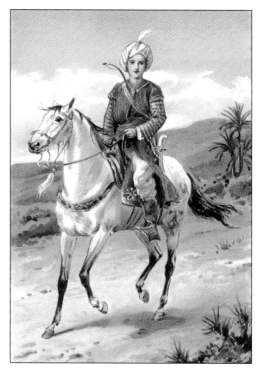
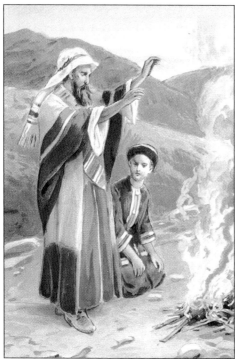
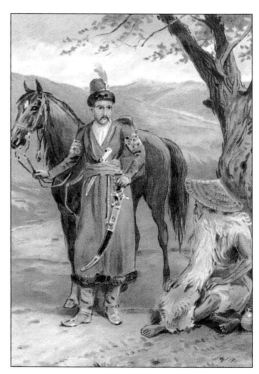

Top left: "She got up in her turn, and taking the stick …"
Top right: "He was mounted upon a white horse, having a golden bridle and shod with gold"
Bottom left: "A thick and dense smoke immediately arose, which seemed to unfold itself in consequence of some mysterious words …"
Bottom right: "He advanced towards the dervise, while he held his horse by the bridle …"

A. W. Cooper, 1902

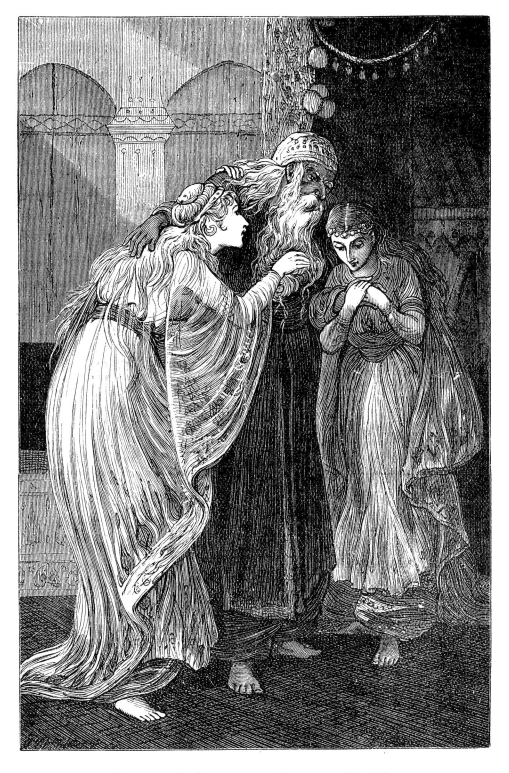

The Vizier's daughter entreating the consent of her father

Thomas B. Dalziel, 1902

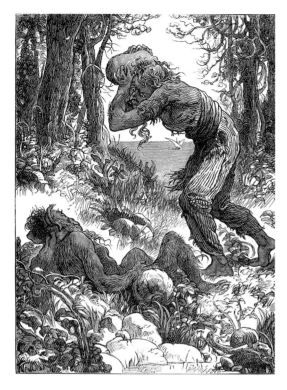

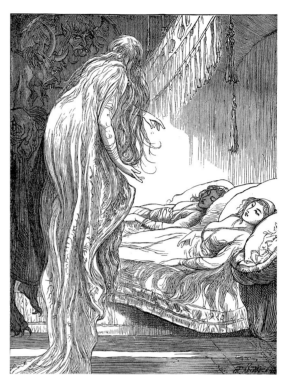

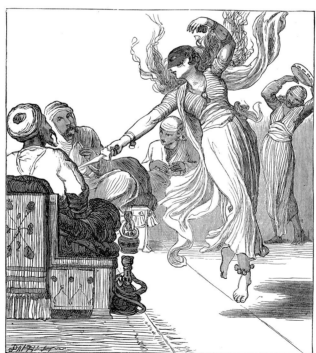

Top left: The Old Man of the Sea
Top right: Comparison
Bottom: Morgiana

Thomas B. Dalziel, 1902

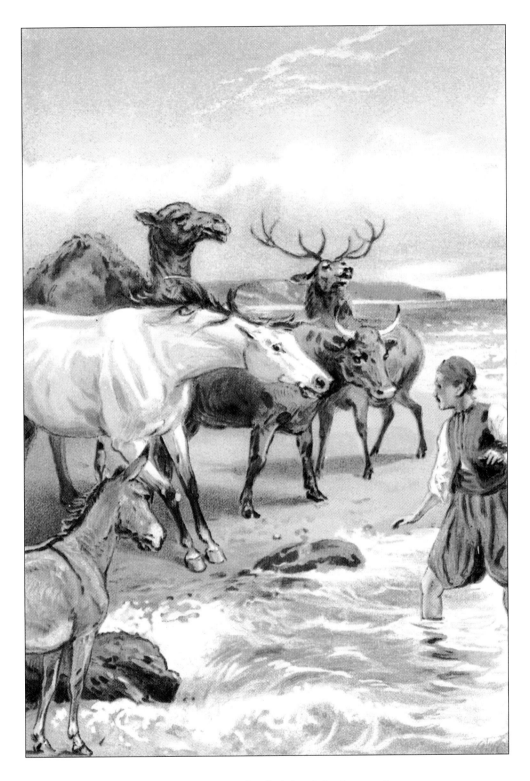

"...and other animals, which lined the shore, and
put themselves in a posture to prevent his landing"

A. W. Cooper, 1902

Opposite: The Princess burns the Efrite to death

Edmund Dulac, 1914

Edmund Dulac

Stories from The Arabian Nights, 1907
Sindbad the Sailor; and Other Stories
from the Arabian Nights, 1914

After Arthur Rackham, Edmund Dulac is perhaps the best known and appreciated of the Golden Age illustrators. Dulac, born in Toulouse, France, in 1882, moved to his adopted England in 1904. Like René Bull, he had a particular affection for and familiarity with Eastern subjects and styles. While Dulac was a child, his father had traveled widely, bringing prints from the East for the young Edmund to copy. An opportunity to work on his own extensive version of the Arabian Nights came in 1907, and the brilliant young illustrator used it to showcase his talent. The success of the volume for Hodder and Stoughton in London assured Dulac employment in gift books for years to come, and he returned to Arabian Nights themes in 1913 *(Princess Badoura)* and 1914 *(Sinbad the Sailor)*. In later years Dulac designed stamps and documents for France, England, and other European countries. Dulac died in England in 1953.

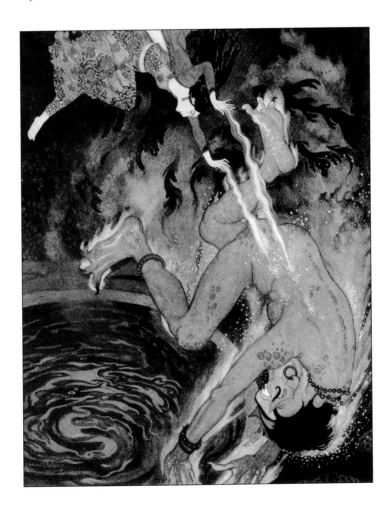

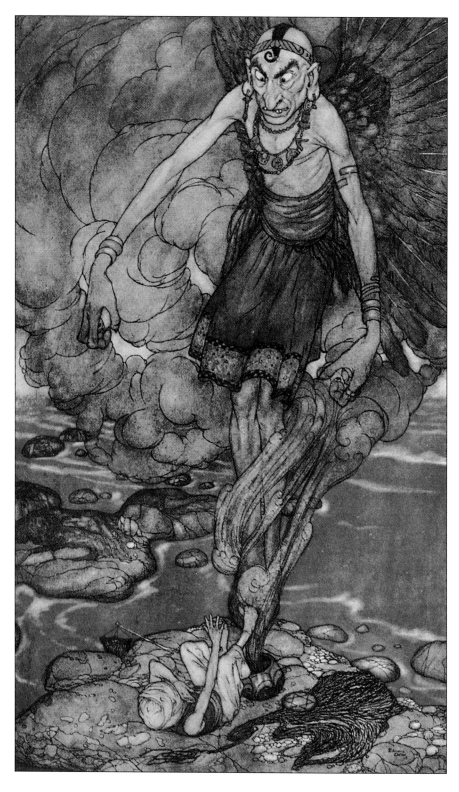

And there in its midst stood a mighty Genie

Edmund Dulac, 1907

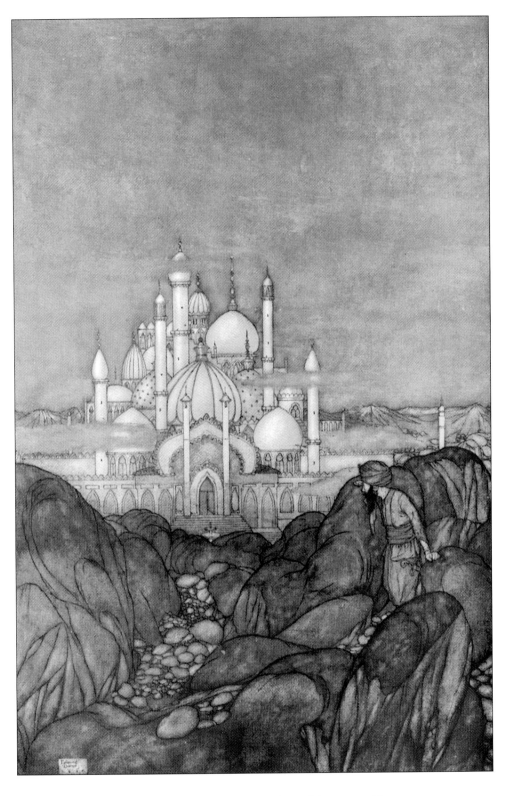

He arrived within sight of a palace of shining marble

Edmund Dulac, 1907

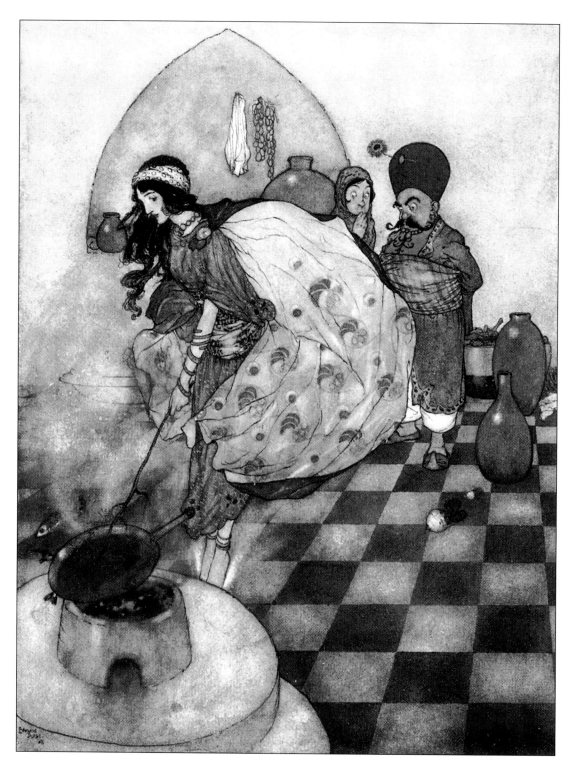

Whereupon one upset the pan into the fire

Edmund Dulac, 1907

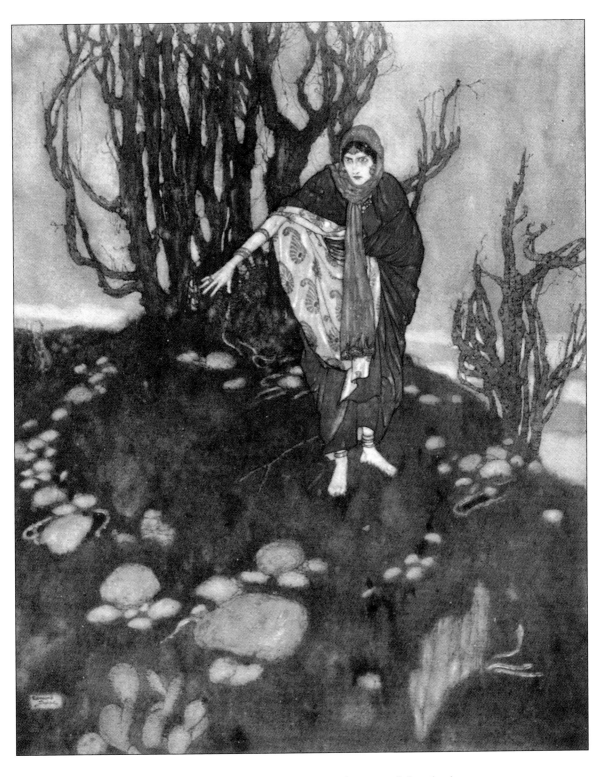

She went on to vent her malice upon the city and the islands

Edmund Dulac, 1907

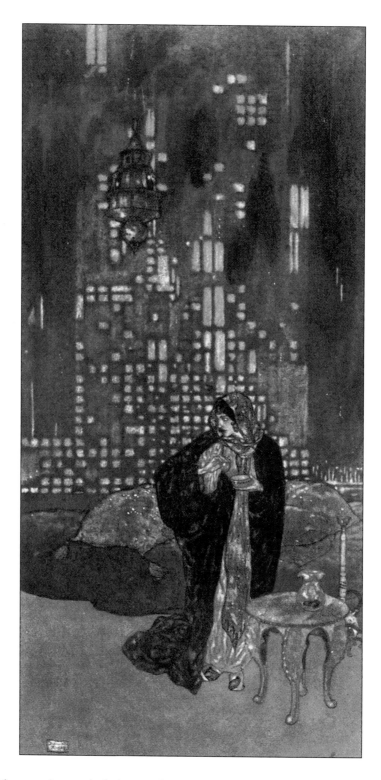

The cup of wine which she gives him each night contains a sleeping-draught

Edmund Dulac, 1907

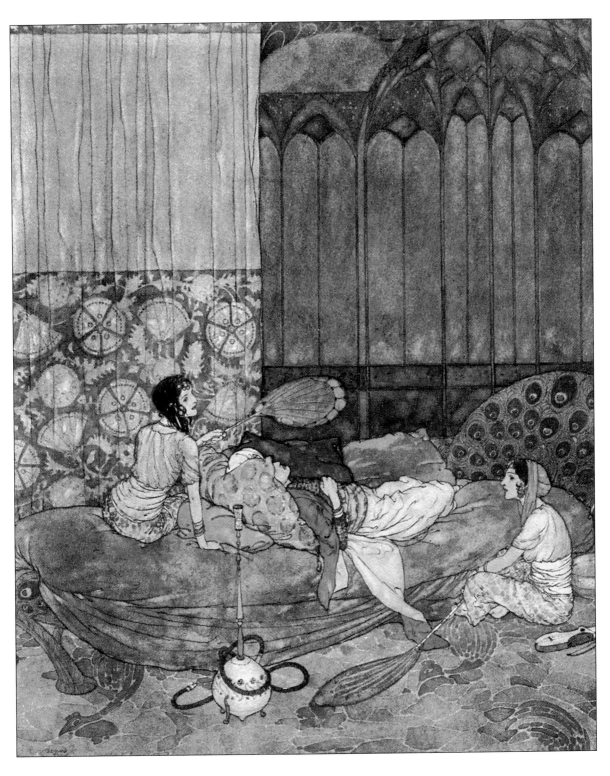

Supposing me asleep they began to talk

Edmund Dulac, 1907

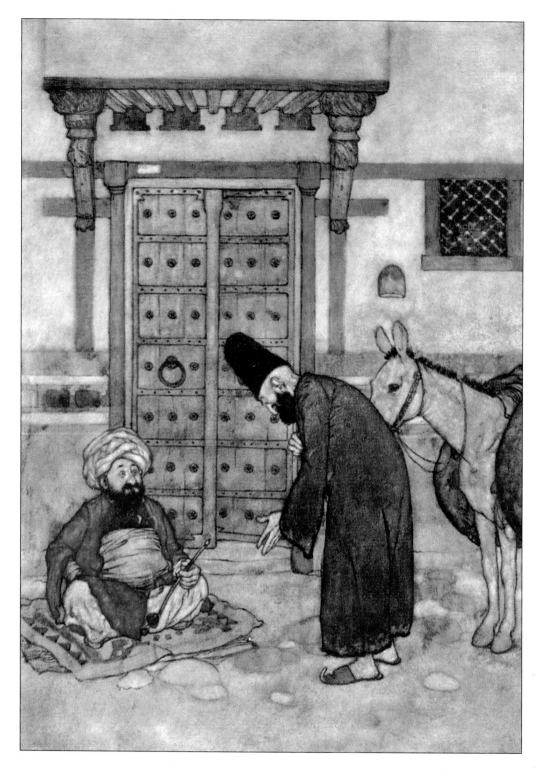

"Sir," said he, "I have brought my oil a great distance to sell to-morrow"

Edmund Dulac, 1907

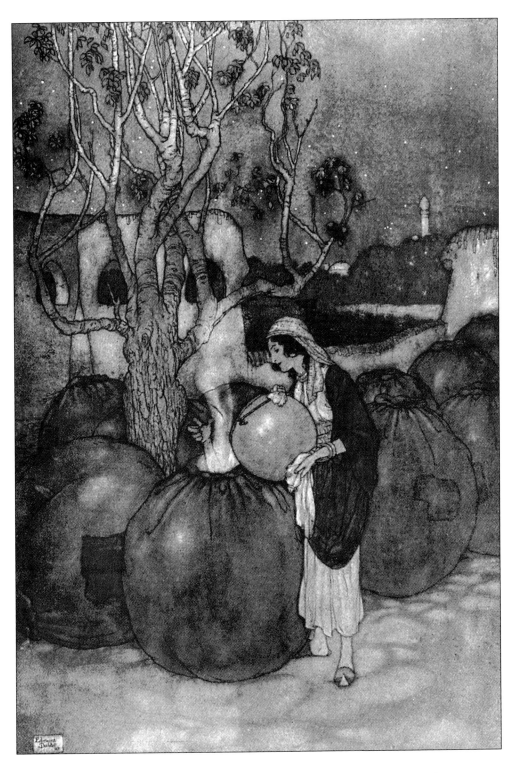

She poured into each jar in turn a sufficient quantity of the boiling oil
to scald its occupant to death

Edmund Dulac, 1907

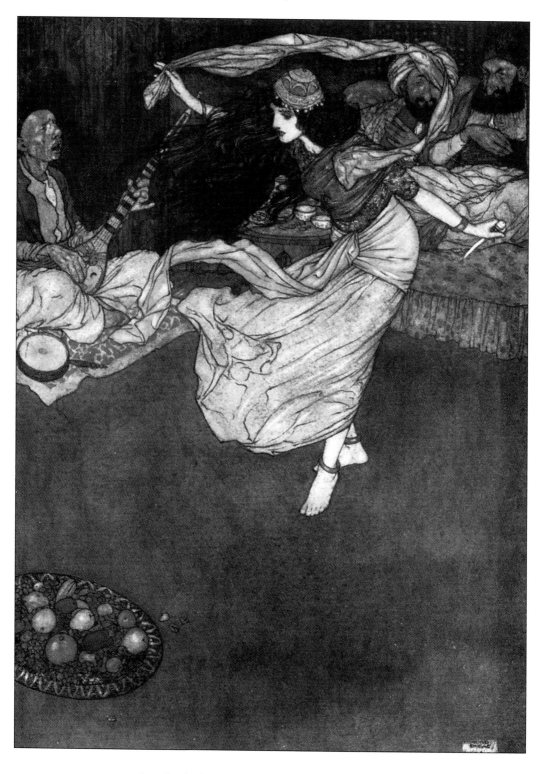

Then for the last figure of all she drew out the dagger

Edmund Dulac, 1907

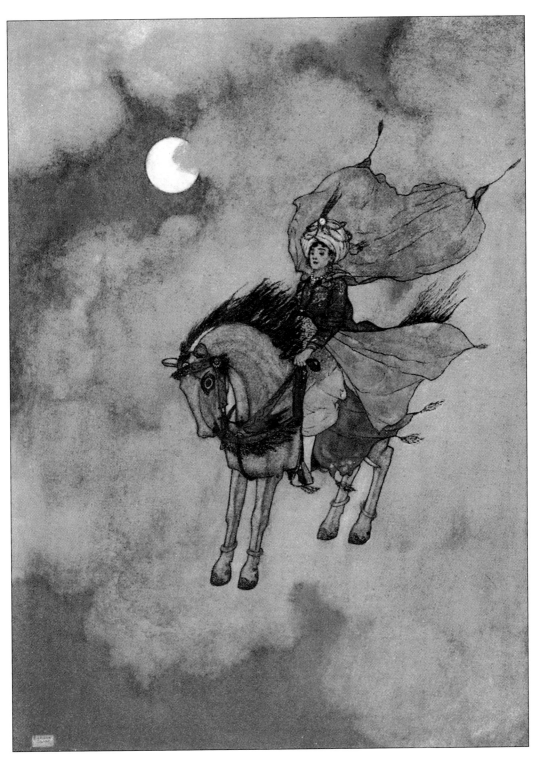

As he descended, the daylight in which hitherto he had been travelling faded from view

Edmund Dulac, 1907

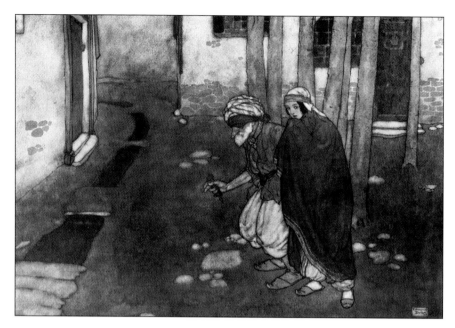

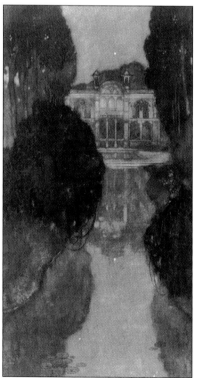

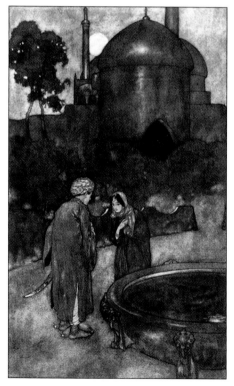

Top: This way and that she led him blindfold
Bottom left: In the garden of the summer palace all was silence and solitude
Bottom right: The lady advanced to meet him

Edmund Dulac, 1907

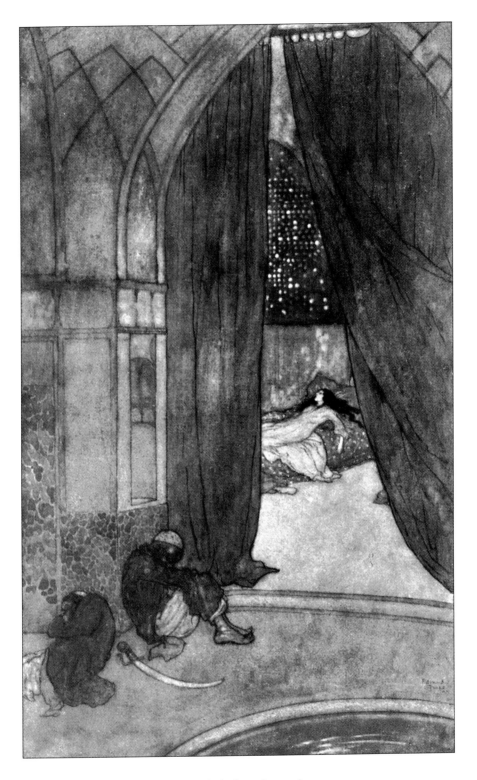

He saw black slaves lying asleep

Edmund Dulac, 1907

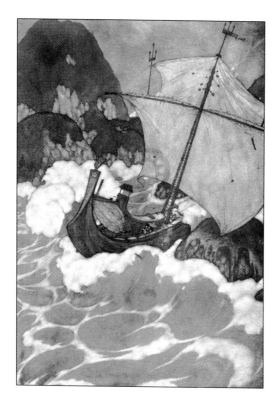

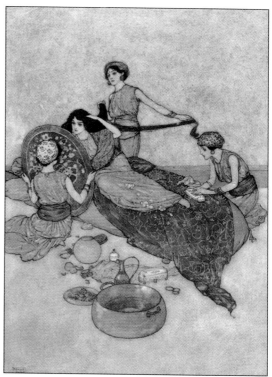

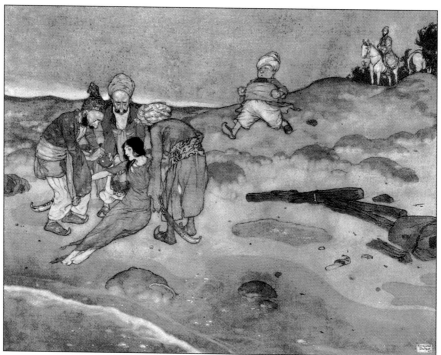

Top left: The ship struck upon a rock
Top right: Till the tale of her mirror contented her
Bottom: And presently, feeling myself lifted by men's hands

Edmund Dulac, 1907

54

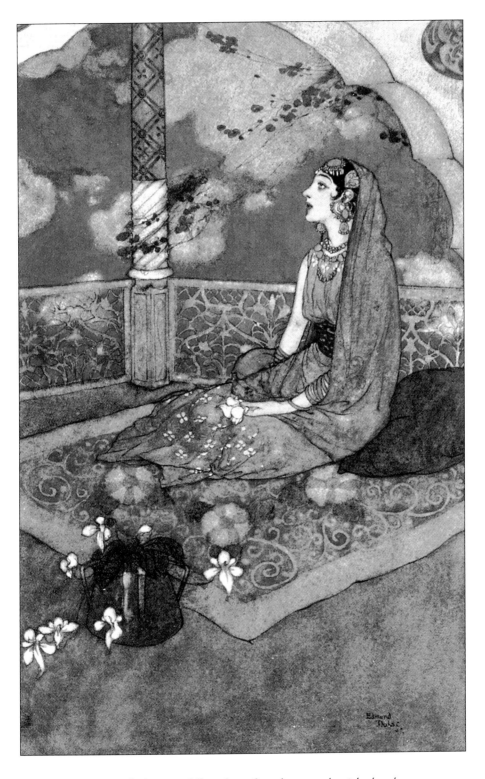

And ever with the tears falling down from her eyes she sighed and sang

Edmund Dulac, 1907

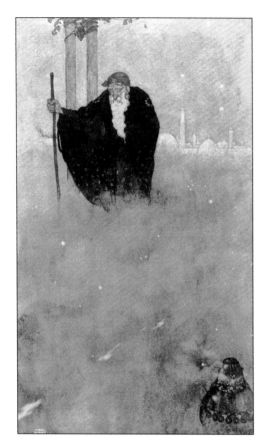
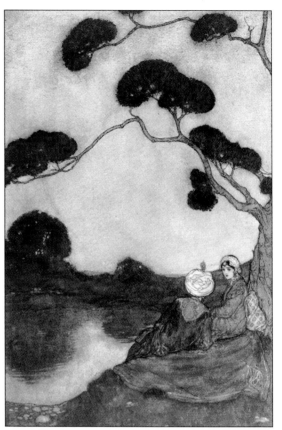
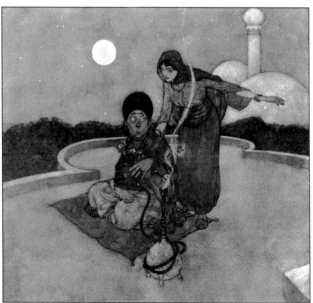

Top left: There appeared before him an old man of venerable appearance
Top right: Sat by the lake and solaced themselves sweetly with love
Bottom: She cried: "O miserable man, what sorry watch is this that thou hast kept"

Edmund Dulac, 1907

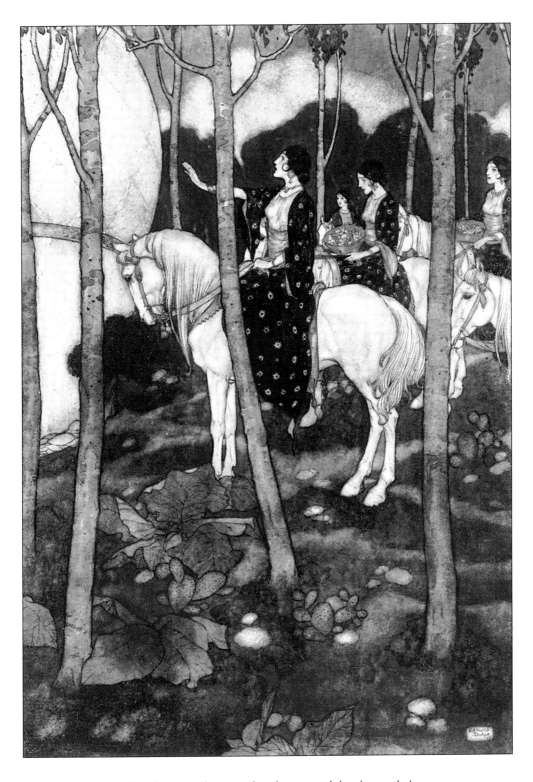

After these, maidens on white horses, with heads unveiled,
bearing in their hands baskets of precious stones

Edmund Dulac, 1907

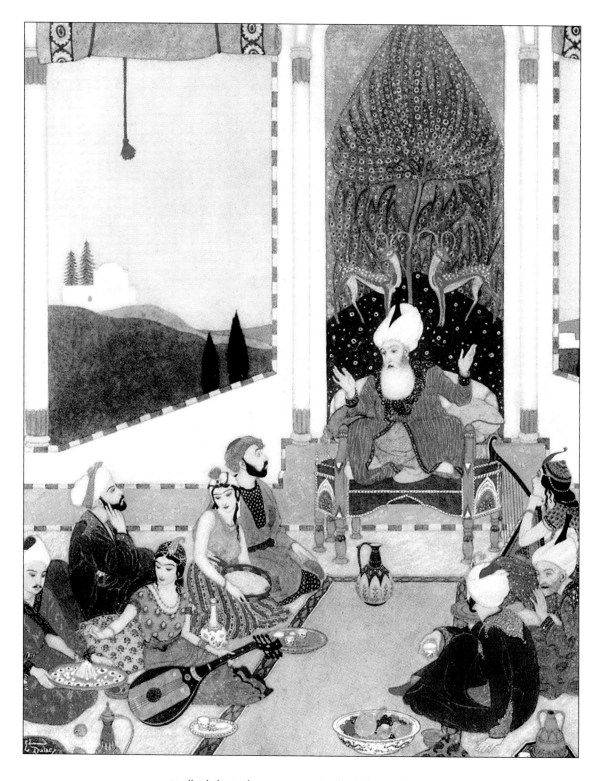

Sindbad the Sailor entertains Sindbad the Landsman

Edmund Dulac, 1914

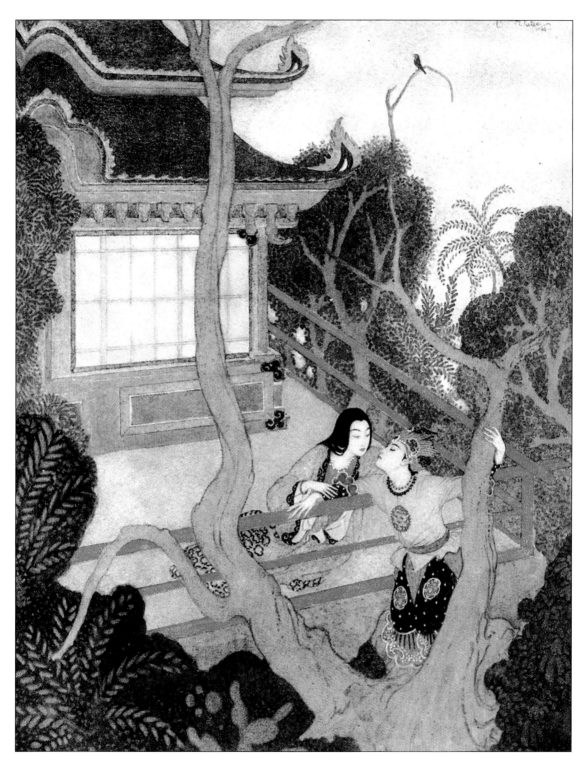

Aladdin finds the Princess in Africa

Edmund Dulac, 1914

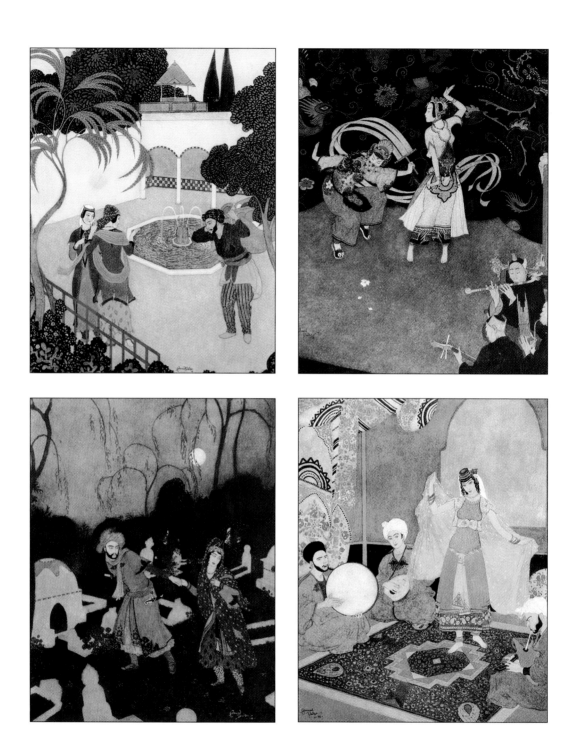

Top left: The Porter and the Ladies
Top right: The Nuptial Dance of Aladdin and the Lady Bedr-el-Budur
Bottom left: The Prince leads the Lady to the Tomb
Bottom right: Abu-l-Hasan entertains the strangers with dancing and music

Edmund Dulac, 1914

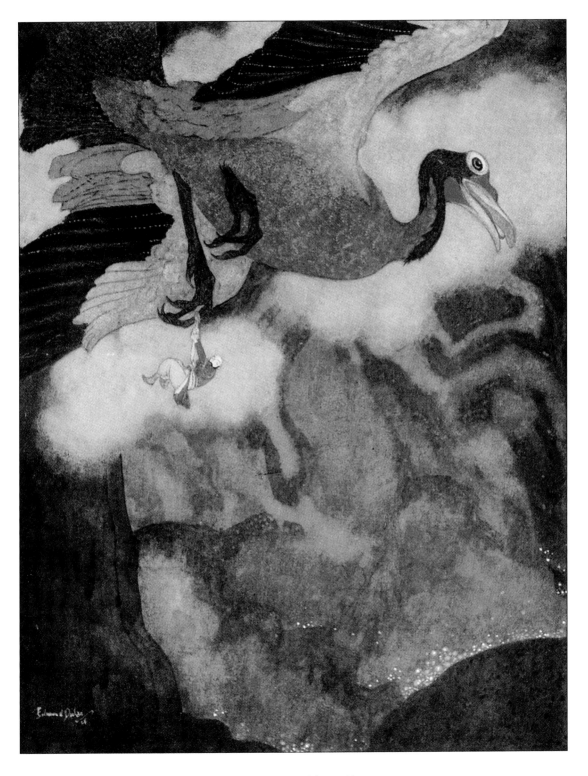

The Episode of the Rokh

Edmund Dulac, 1914

Opposite left: "Brother, I cannot part from you without desiring you
to consider once more how difficult a thing it is
to govern thirty loaded camels"
Opposite right: Chapter decorations

Charles Folkard, 1913

Charles Folkard
The Arabian Nights, 1913

As an illustrator of children's books, Charles Folkard (1878–1963) possessed a long and enviable list of titles, but he was equally well known for his work on a British newspaper comic, *The Adventures of Teddy Tail* (considered by many to be a predecessor to Mickey Mouse). Among Folkard's earliest books was a liberally illustrated edition of *Pinocchio*, which became the definitive edition. His *Arabian Nights*, published in 1913, was one in a group of books he produced in a long-lasting and successful relationship with A. & C. Black. An active illustrator to the end of his days, Folkard continually worked with and returned to the subjects of nursery rhymes and children's tales.

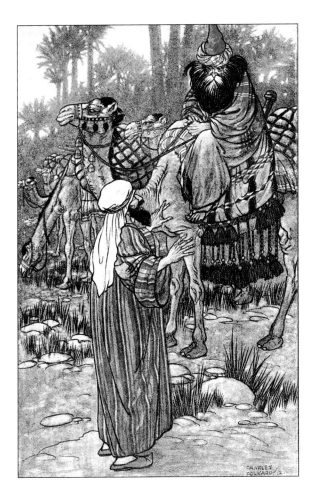

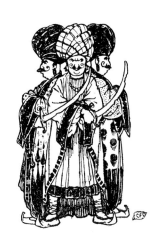

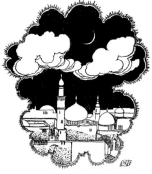

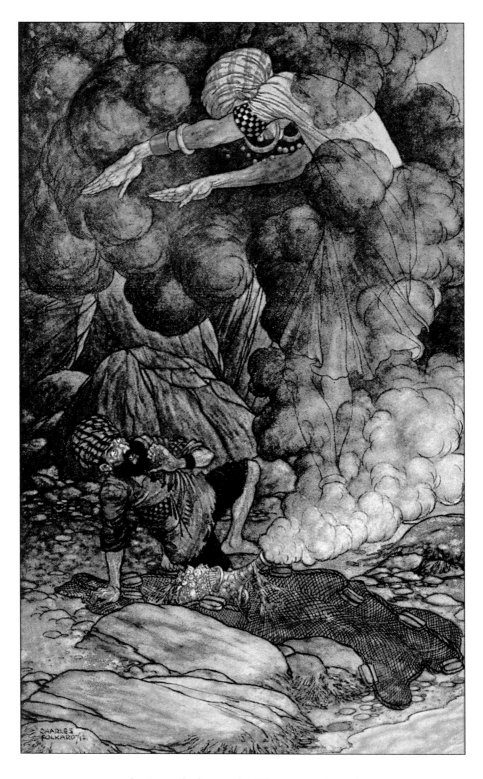

The Genie, looking at the fisherman, exclaimed:
"Humble thyself before me, or I will kill thee"

Charles Folkard, 1913

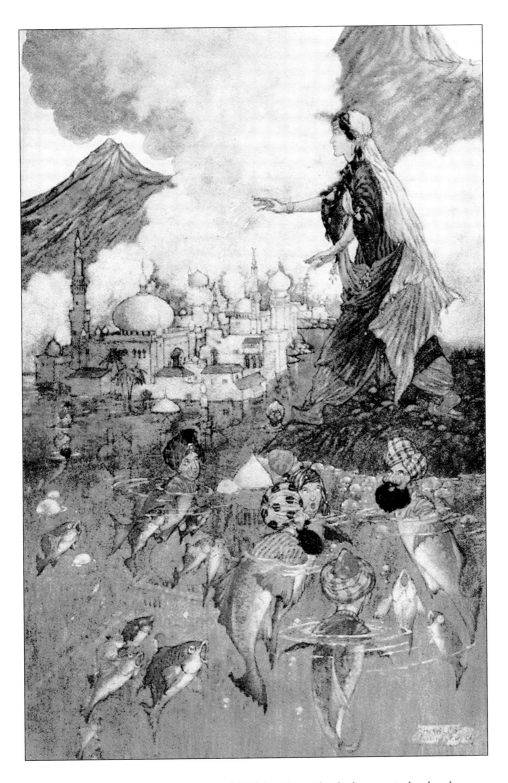

"When she came to the border of the lake, she took a little water in her hand,
and scattered it about . . . The fish became men, women, and children"

Charles Folkard, 1913

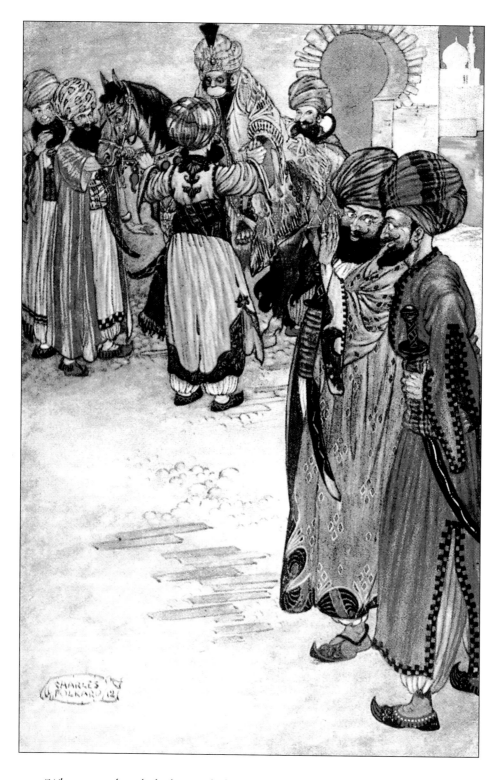

"Whereupon they clothed me with the rich brocade robe, and carried me ashore,
where they set me on horseback"

Charles Folkard, 1913

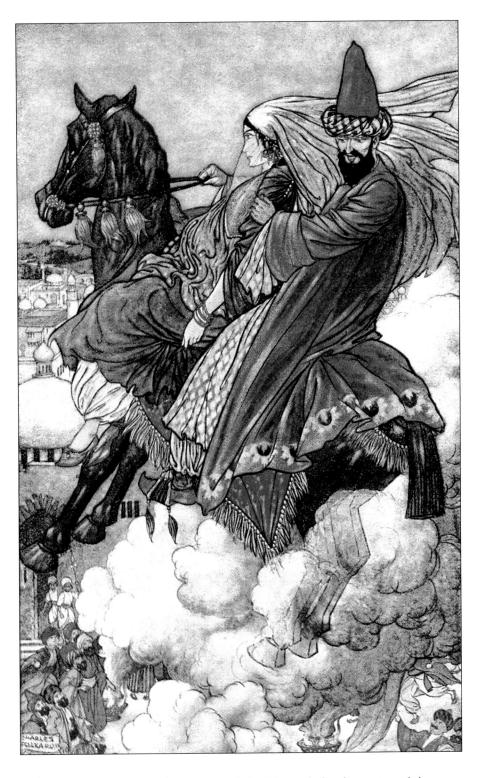

"The Hindu ... mounted on his horse, took the Princess before him ... turned the peg,
and instantly the horse mounted into the air"

Charles Folkard, 1913

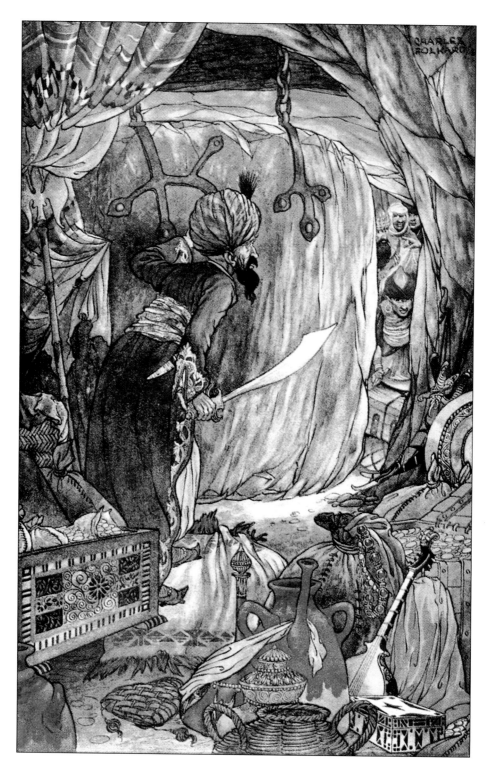

"Cassim . . . resolved to make one effort for his life"

Charles Folkard, 1913

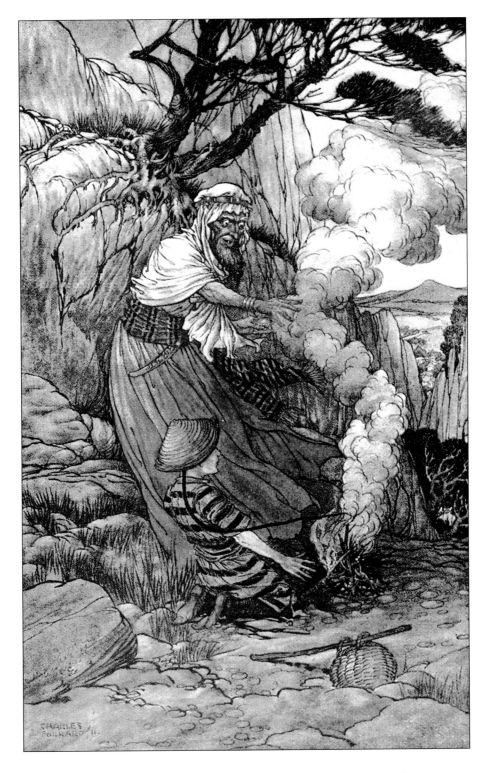

"The Magician presently set them on fire; and when they were in a blaze,
threw in some incense"

Charles Folkard, 1913

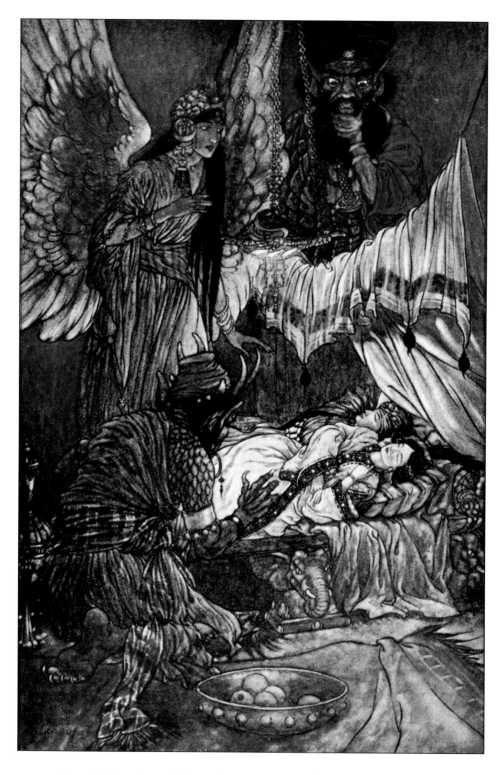

"Rise, Caschcasch," said she, "and cast your eye on that bed, and tell us truly
which is the most beautiful, this prince or this princess"

Charles Folkard, 1913

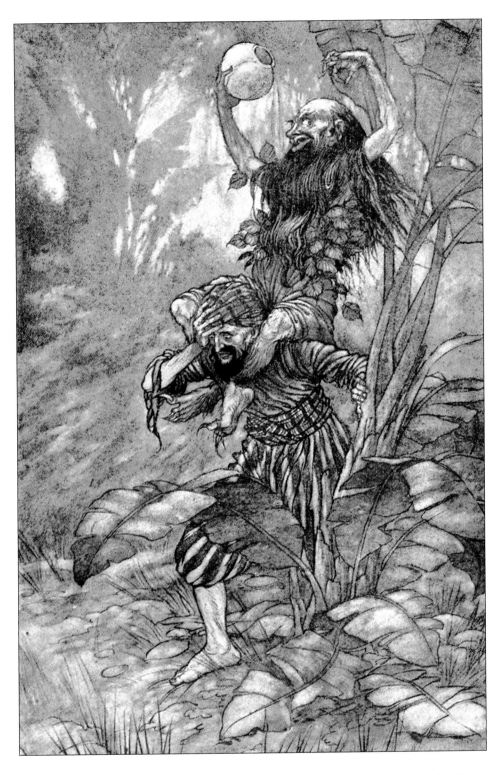

"He soon began to sing, and to move about from side to side in his seat upon my shoulders, and by degrees to loosen his legs from about me"

Charles Folkard, 1913

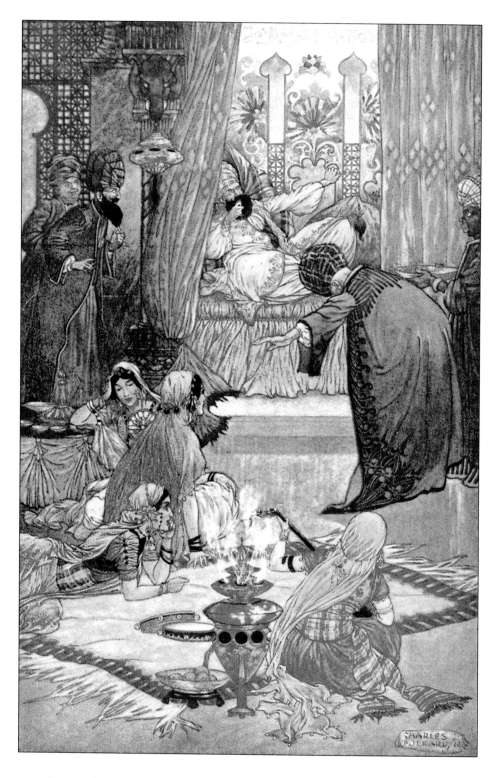

"Commander of the Faithful, your Majesty will excuse me for representing to you,
that you used not to rise so late"

Charles Folkard, 1913

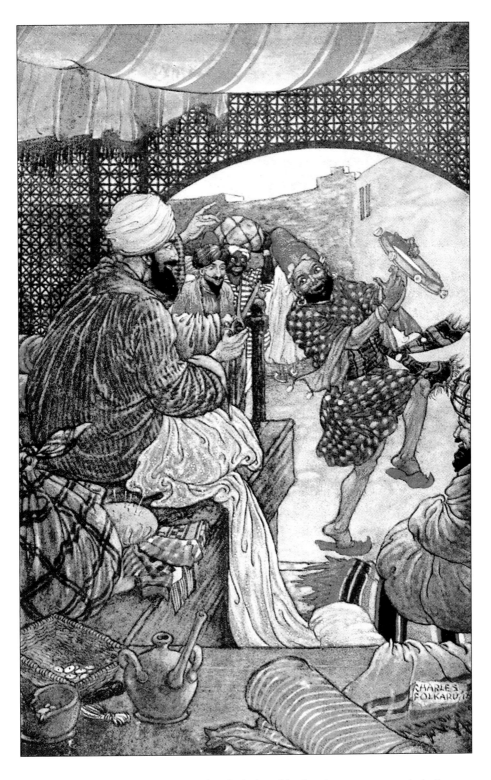

"One day, while he was at work, a little hunchback...began to sing and play"

Charles Folkard, 1913

Opposite: Agib entertained by the ladies

H. J. Ford, 1898

h. J. Ford
The Arabian Nights Entertainments, 1898

A consummate draftsman and inker, Henry Justice Ford (1860–1940) primarily is remembered for his stunning illustration work on a twelve-volume set of "fairy books"—each titled with a different color—from around the world, collected and edited by Andrew Lang. This body of work kept Ford employed for twenty years; the first, *The Blue Fairy Book*, was published in 1889, and the last, *The Lilac Fairy Book*, appeared in 1910. Ford was a friend of the Pre-Raphaelite painter Sir Edward Burne-Jones, who shared his vision of romance in his visual storytelling. Ford's work on *The Arabian Nights Entertainments* was very much in keeping with his illustrations in Lang's Fairy Books, both in style and format. These books are in print today, largely due to the appeal of Ford's skilled renderings.

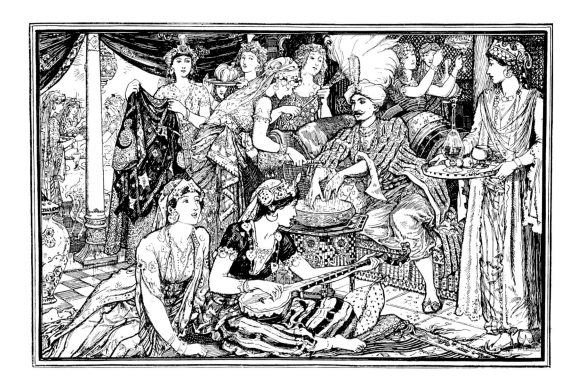

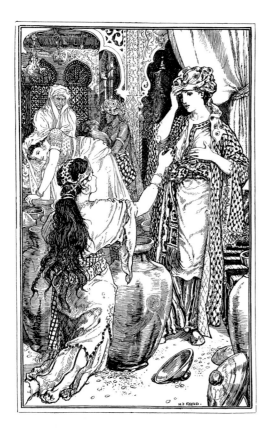

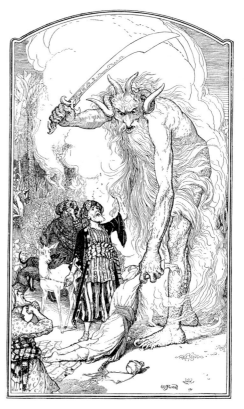

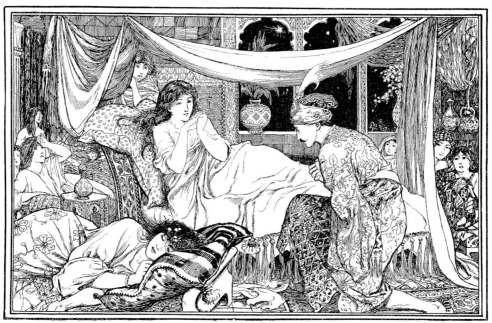

Top left: The talisman is discovered in one of the jars
Top right: The genius and the merchants
Bottom: Prince Firouz Schah in the chamber of the princess of Bengal

H. J. Ford, 1898

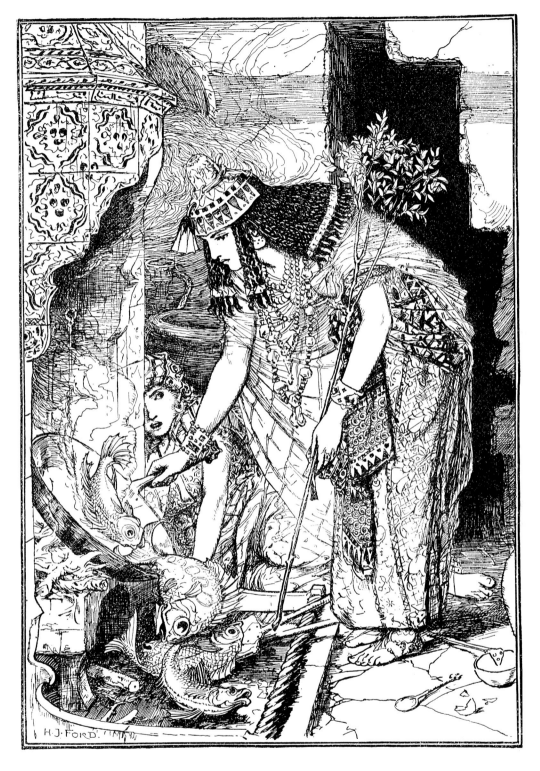

The girl upsets the frying-pan

H. J. Ford, 1898

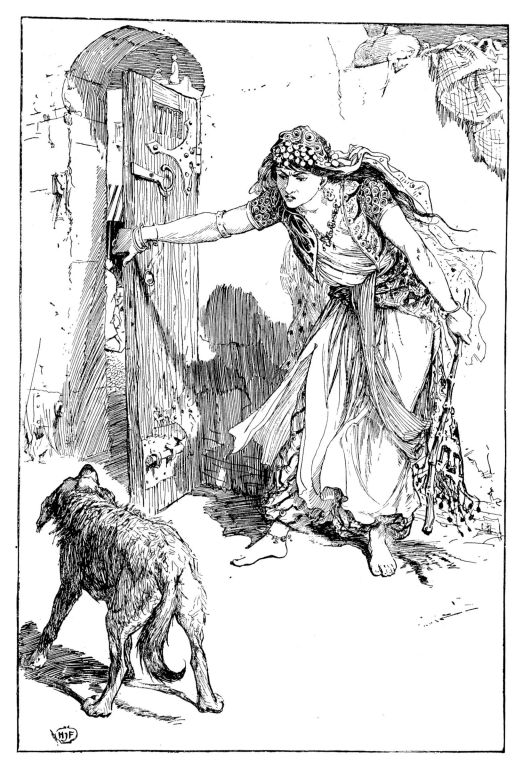

She opened the gate, intending to crush me as I passed through

H. J. Ford, 1898

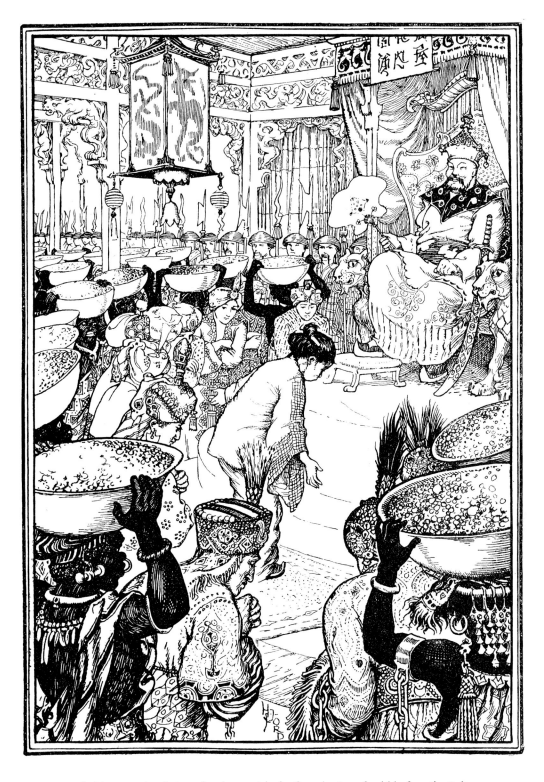

Aladdin's mother brings the slaves with the forty basins of gold before the Sultan

H. J. Ford, 1898

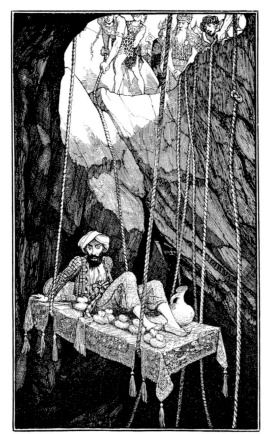

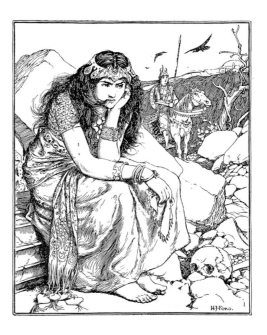

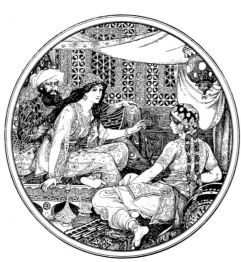

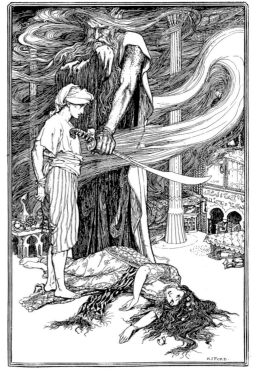

Top left: Sindbad lowered into the cavern

Top right: The prince falls in with the ogress

Bottom left: Scheherazade, Dinarzade, and the Sultan

Bottom right: The genius commands the young man to slay the princess

H. J. Ford, 1898

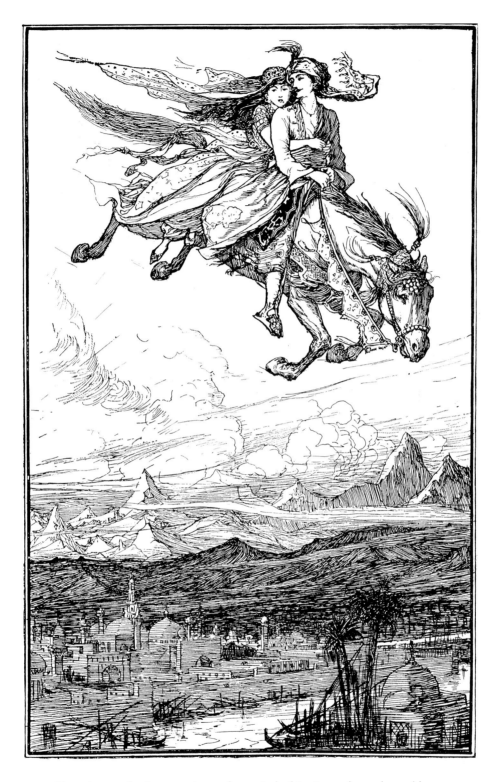

The prince and princess arrive at the capital of Persia on the enchanted horse

H. J. Ford, 1898

Opposite: The Sultan's daughter, Bedrelbood

Thomas Mackenzie, 1920

Thomas Mackenzie
Aladdin and his Wonderful Lamp, 1920

Carrying on a tradition that Aubrey Beardsley, Harry Clarke, and Kay Nielsen
had begun in Art Nouveau book design and illustration, Thomas Mackenzie
(1887–1944) would not equal their fame, but he did produce some true illus-
trative gems. The work Mackenzie did for *Aladdin and his Wonderful Lamp* is
among his very best. Mackenzie studied at the Bradford College of Art, and
later at the Slade, receiving his first commission for bookwork in 1920—
Chaundler's *Arthur and his Knights.*

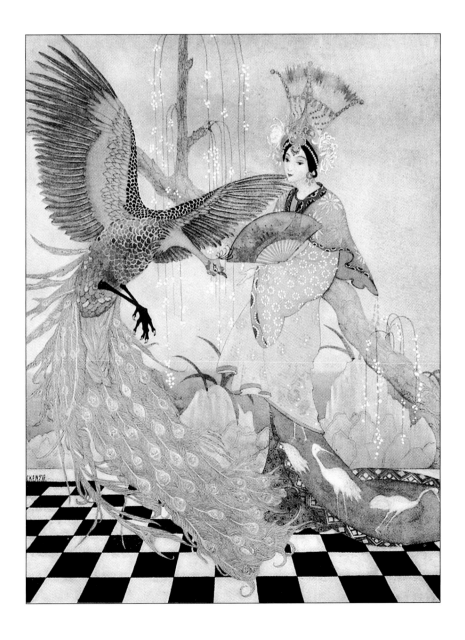

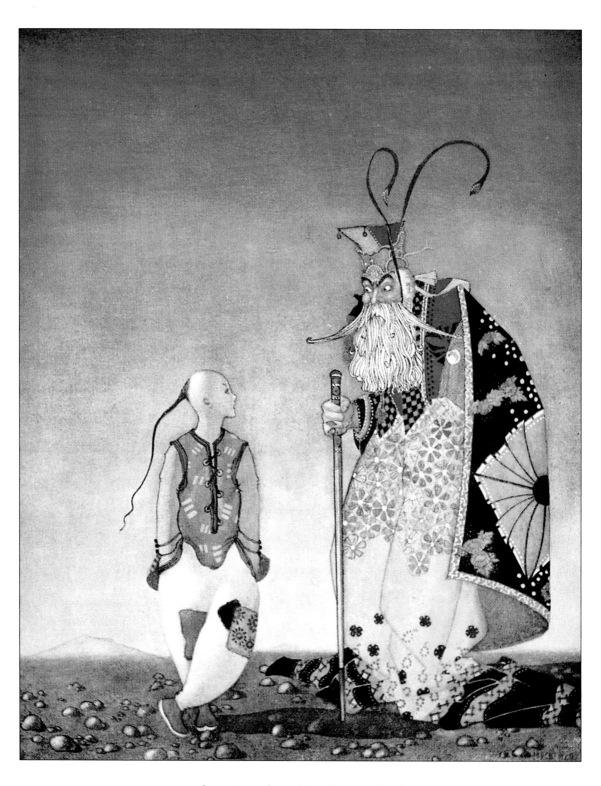

"The man was dressed in yellow and black"

Thomas Mackenzie, 1920

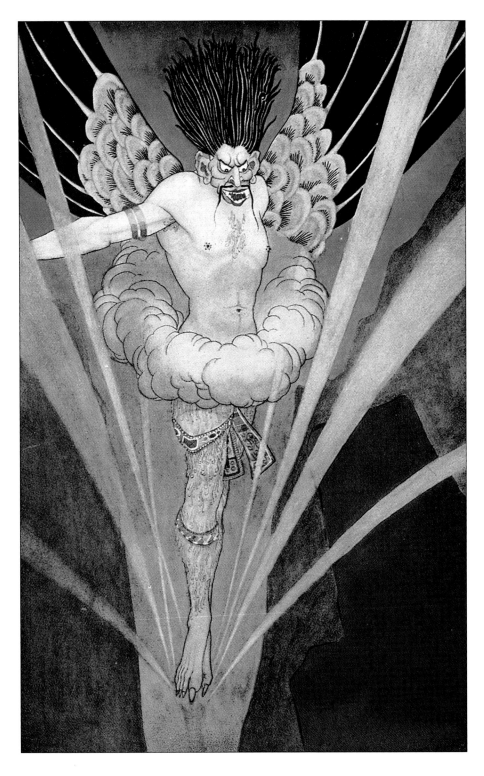

The Slave of the Lamp

Thomas Mackenzie, 1920

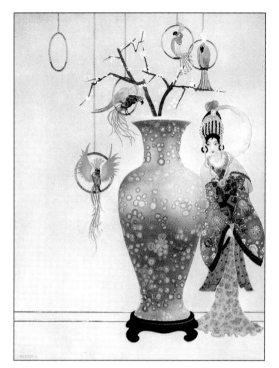
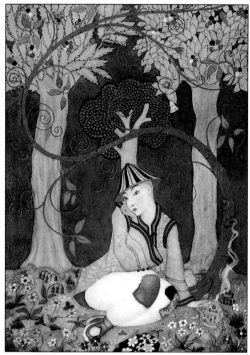
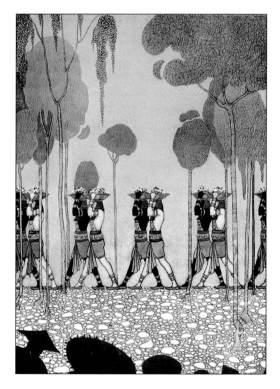
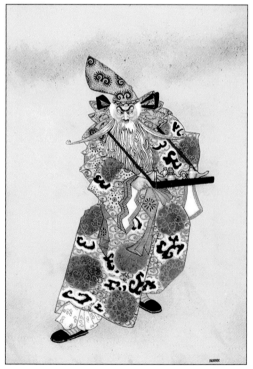

Top left: "His only thought was love and pride in Princess Bedrelbood, his bride"
Top right: "And sobbing he sat under the tree"
Bottom left: "And twelve tall negroes, black as coals, and twelve tall slaves, Circassian, white"
Bottom right: "New lamps for old do I supply"

Thomas Mackenzie, 1920

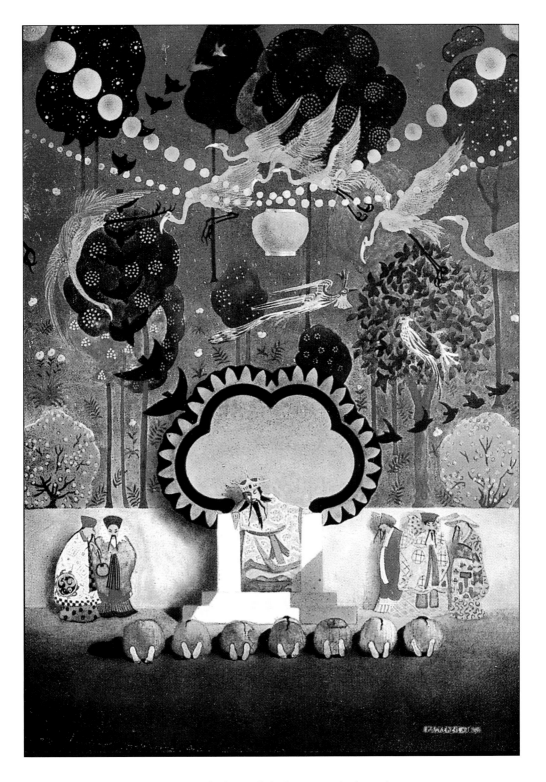

"...A crowd of pig-taled Chinamen who bowed"

Thomas Mackenzie, 1920

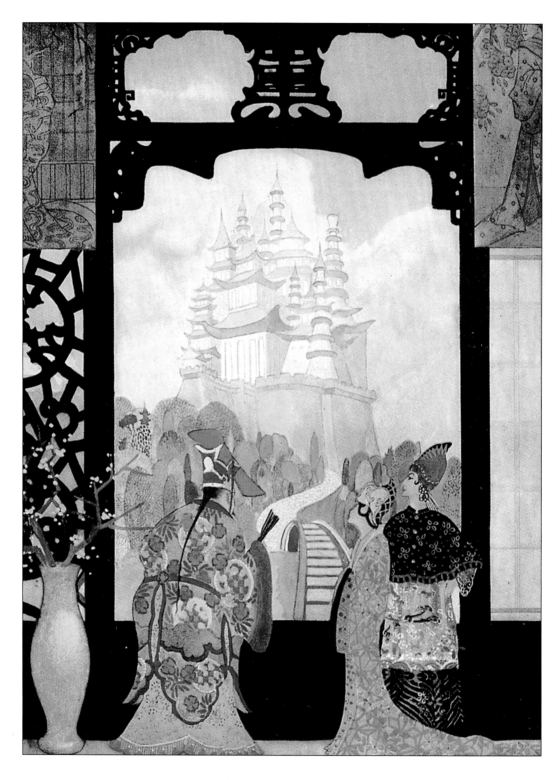

"Of all miraculous surprises"

Thomas Mackenzie, 1920

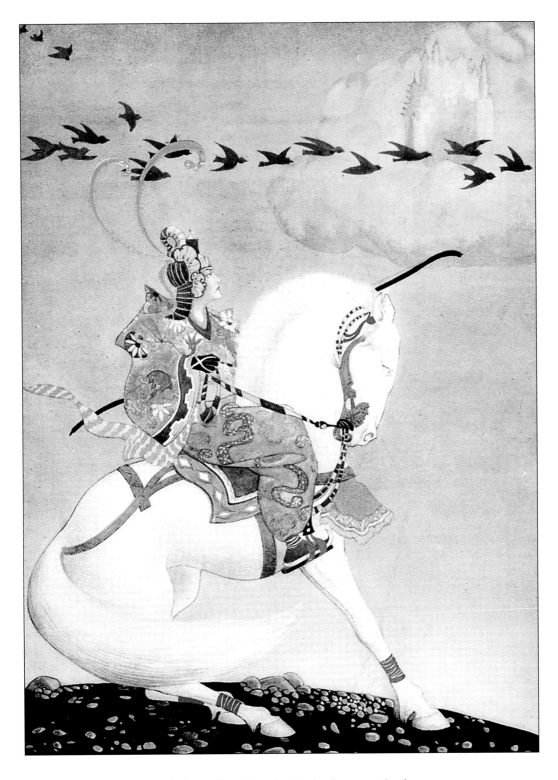

...'Tis little good to chase the deeds of magic with a horse

Thomas Mackenzie, 1920

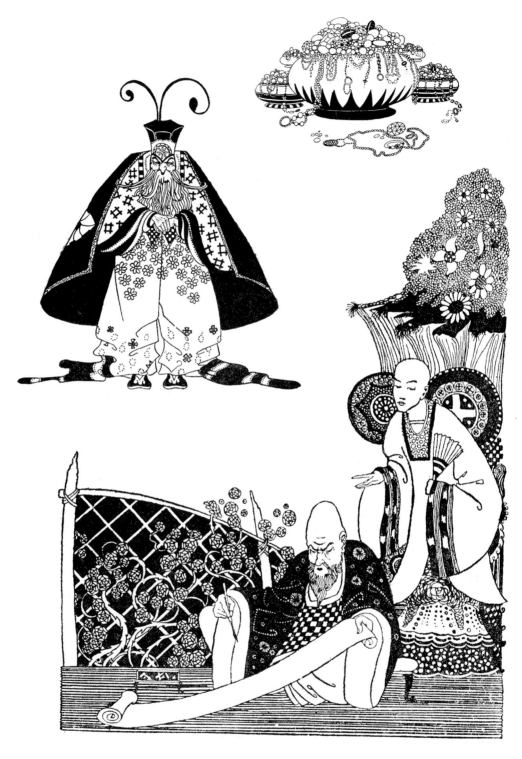

Various line decorations

Thomas Mackenzie, 1920

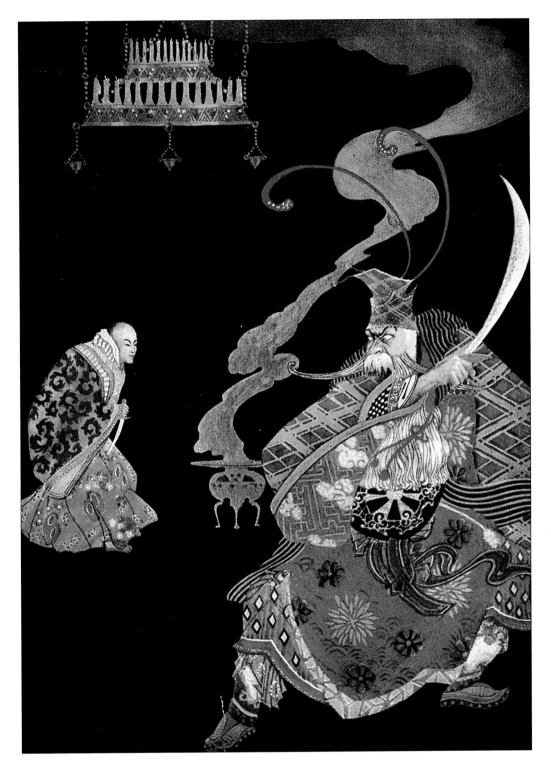

"The Magician struck, but his blows fell wide"

Thomas Mackenzie, 1920

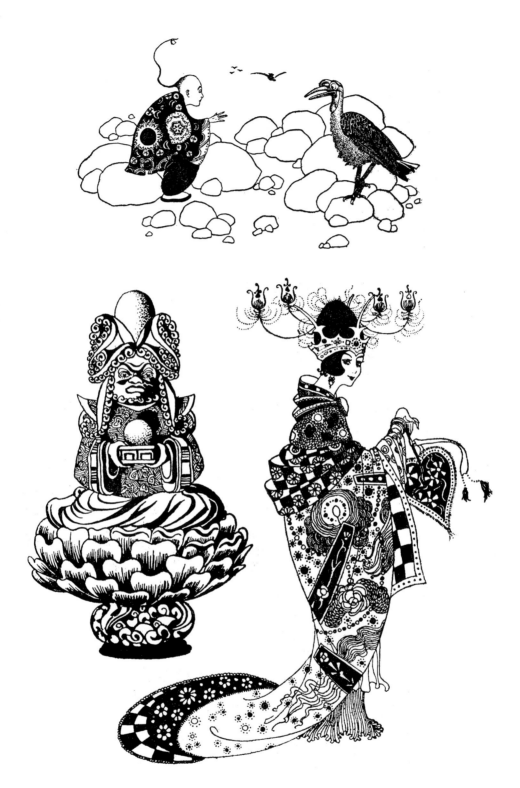

Various line decorations

Thomas Mackenzie, 1920

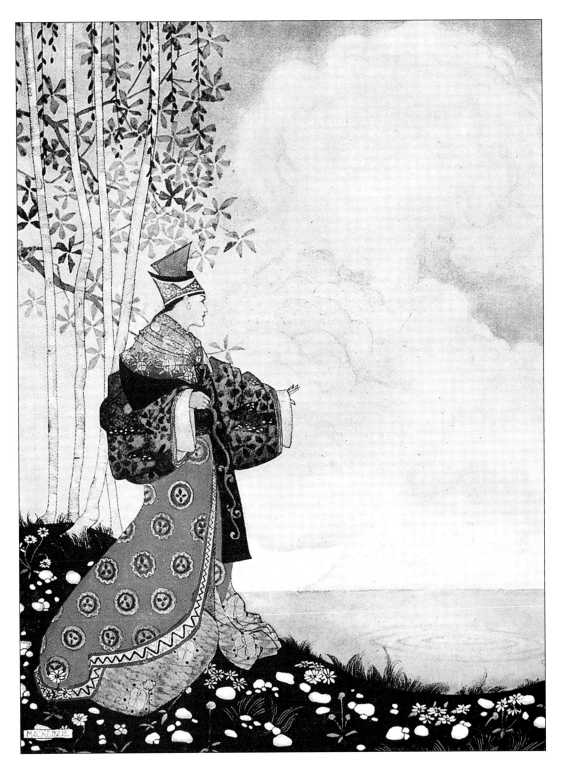

"He flung far out the talisman"

Thomas Mackenzie, 1920

Opposite: THE CITY OF BRASS
And when they had ascended that mountain they saw a city
than which eyes had not beheld any greater

Maxfield Parrish, 1909

Maxfield Parrish
The Arabian Nights: Their Best-Known Tales, 1909

Maxfield Parrish (1870–1966) was one of the premier American illustrators of the twentieth century. His work has a unique, almost photographic quality, the result of a combination of his approach to his subjects and his innovative painting techniques, many involving studio or landscape photography. His earliest work was for Frank Baum's *Mother Goose* (1897); shortly thereafter he began a career in high-profile, lucrative advertising work, with magazine and classic bookwork to follow. His Arabian Nights work appeared in 1909. Parrish's distinctive look and his use of "trademark" Parrish blue could be seen everywhere, and his work had tremendous public appeal. In the 1930s, seeking more personal satisfaction from his art, he turned to landscape painting; landscapes were always a prominent feature in his illustrations, and for the next thirty years this was the focus of his attention (though mostly for use in calendars). Parrish's work was highly influential on generations of illustrators to follow.

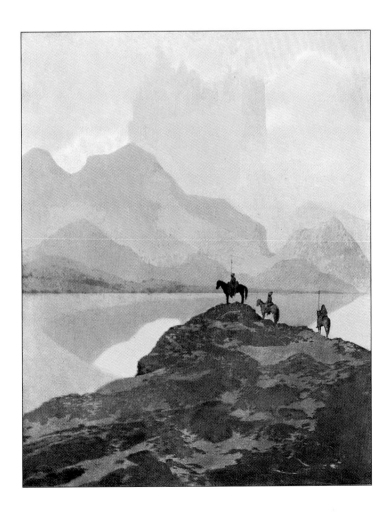

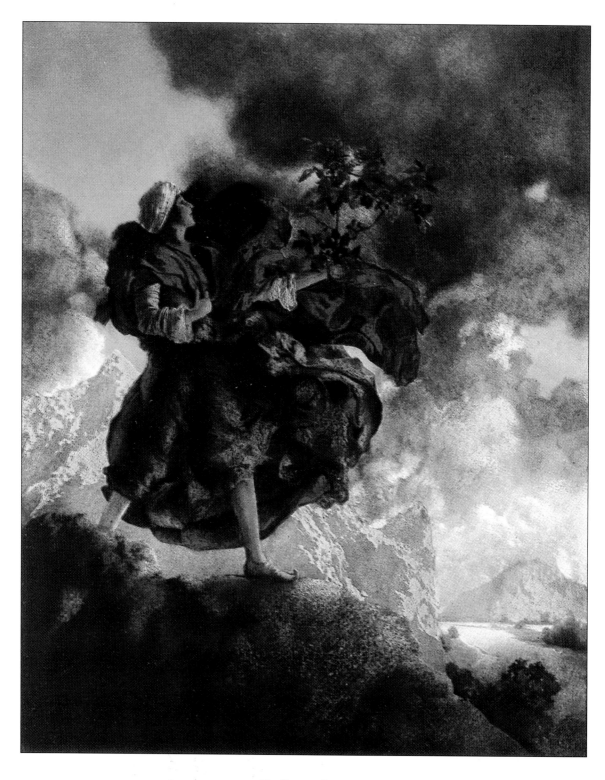

THE TALKING BIRD
It will be sufficient to break off a branch and carry it to plant in your garden

Maxfield Parrish, 1909

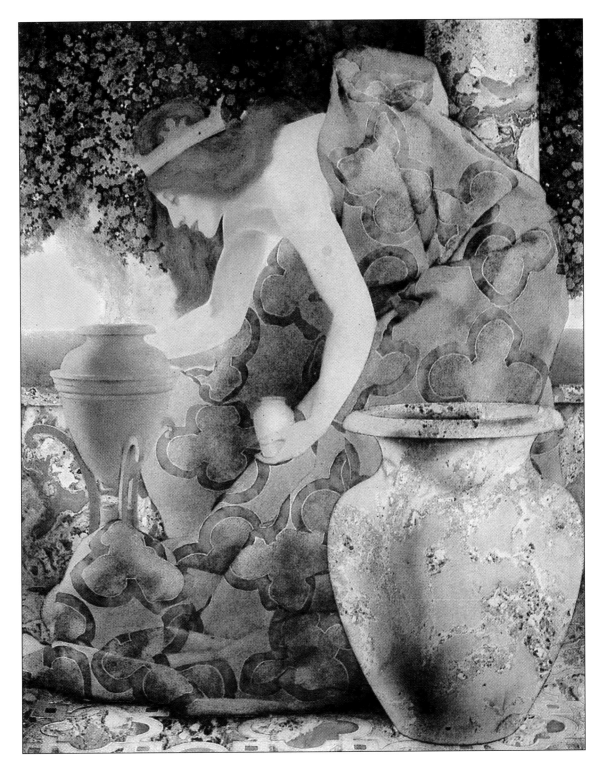

GULNARE OF THE SEA
And she proceeded to burn perfume and repeat spells until the sea foamed and was agitated

Maxfield Parrish, 1909

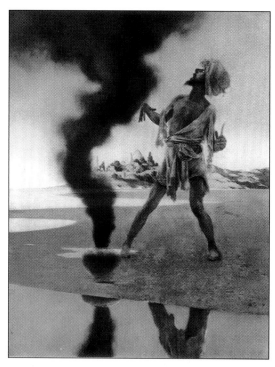
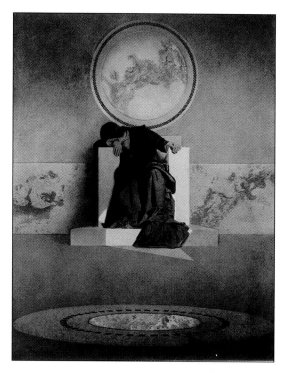
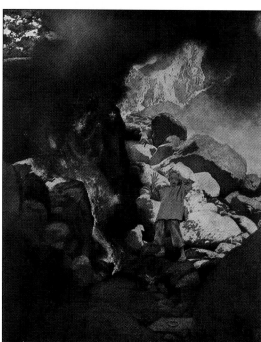
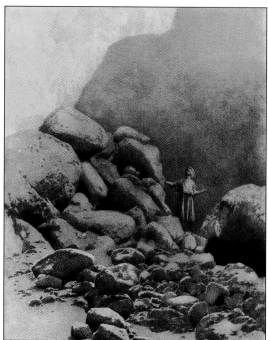

Top left: THE FISHERMAN AND THE GENIE, The smoke ascended to the clouds, and extending itself along the
sea and upon the shore formed a great mist
Top right: THE YOUNG KING OF THE BLACK ISLES, When he came to this part of the narrative
the young king could not restrain his tears
Bottom left: ALADDIN, At the same time the earth, trembling, opened just before the magician,
and uncovered a stone, laid horizontally, with a brass ring fixed into the middle
Bottom right: SECOND VOYAGE OF SINDBAD, The spot where she left me was encompassed on all sides
by mountains that seemed to reach above the clouds,
and so steep that there was no possibility of getting out of the valley

Maxfield Parrish, 1909

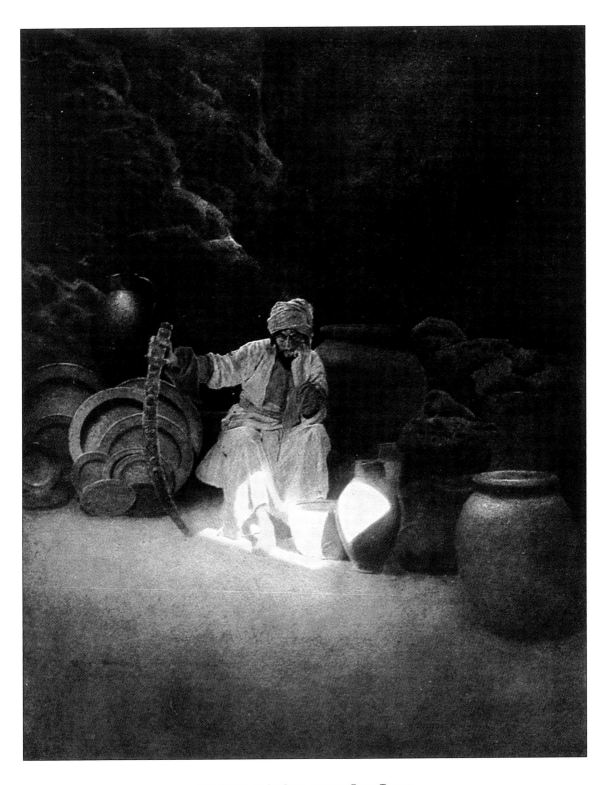

THE STORY OF ALI BABA AND THE FORTY THIEVES
Cassim...was so alarmed at the danger he was in that the more he endeavoured to remember
the word *Sesame* the more his memory was confounded

Maxfield Parrish, 1909

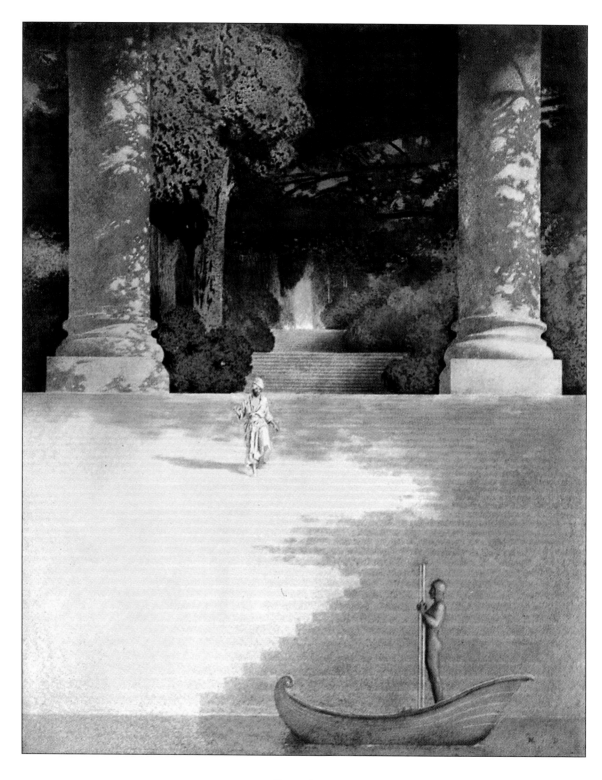

PRINCE AGIB
And when the boat came to me I found in it a man of brass, with a tablet of lead upon his breast,
engraven with names and talismans

Maxfield Parrish, 1909

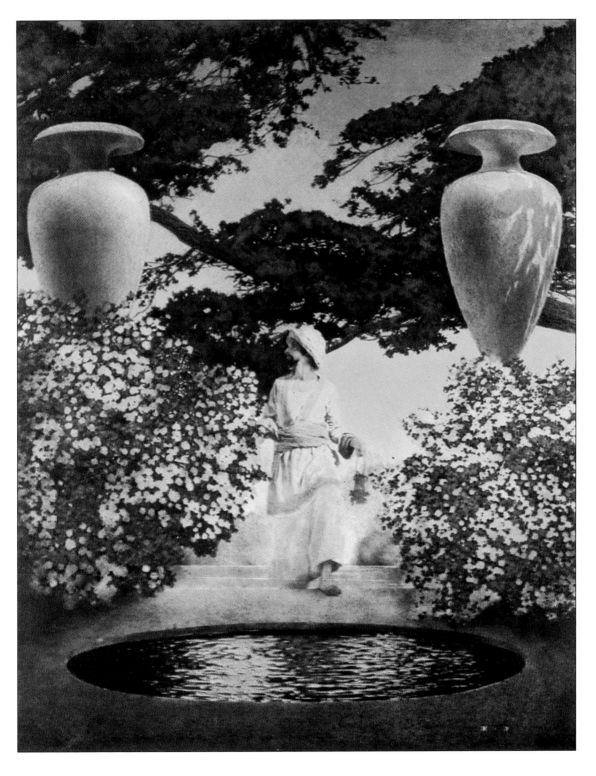

PRINCE AGIB
At the approach of evening I opened the first closet and, entering it, found a mansion like paradise

Maxfield Parrish, 1909

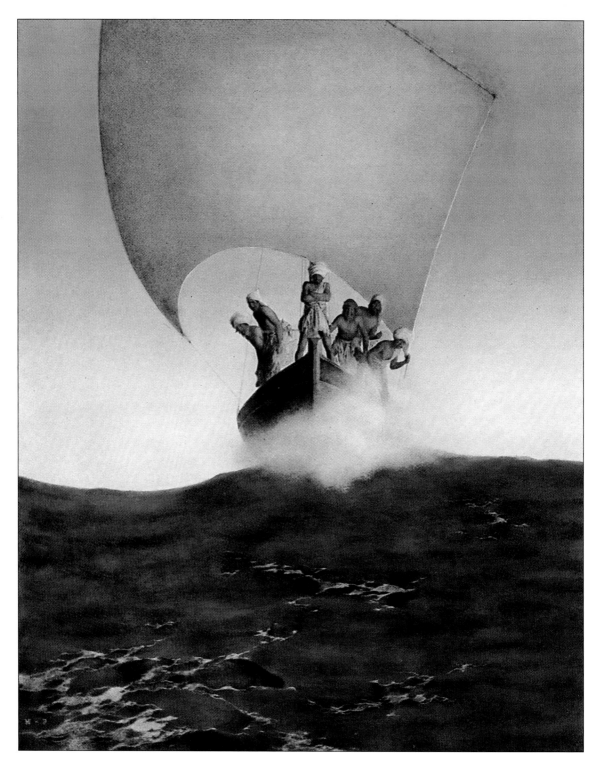

THE HISTORY OF CODADAD AND HIS BROTHERS
As it drew near we saw ten or twelve armed pirates appear on the deck

Maxfield Parrish, 1909

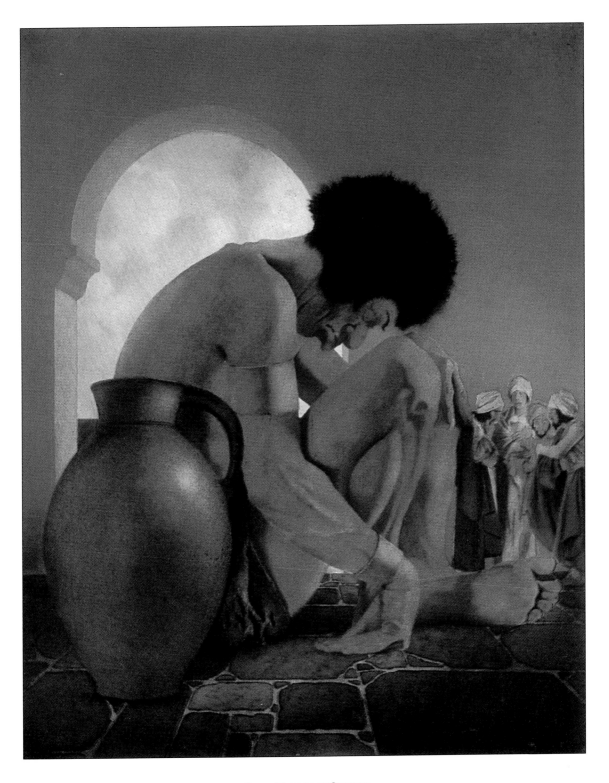

THIRD VOYAGE OF SINDBAD
Having finished his repast, he returned to his porch,
where he lay and fell asleep, snoring louder than thunder

Maxfield Parrish, 1909

Opposite: Contents Headpiece

Louis Rhead, 1916

Louis Rhead

The Arabian Nights' Entertainments, 1916

British-born illustrator Louis Rhead (1858–1926) was still a student in Paris when the New York publisher D. Appleton offered him the post of art director. Earlier years encompassed a wide range of artistic paths—from ceramic design to poster work—but Rhead began to focus more and more on the illustrated book. After 1900, Rhead worked on a great many classic tales, from *Swiss Family Robinson* to *Robin Hood* to *Treasure Island*. His specialty was producing many images in line-art style, rather than executing a handful of paintings. Some of Rhead's projects have more than one hundred drawings, with a decorative element or drawing on nearly every spread. Louis occasionally worked with either or both of his brothers, George Wooliscroft Rhead and Frederick Rhead.

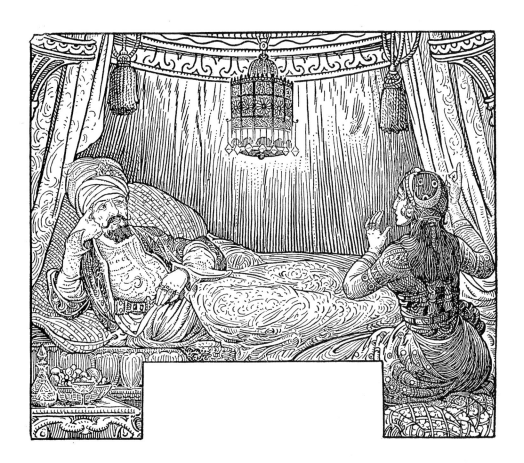

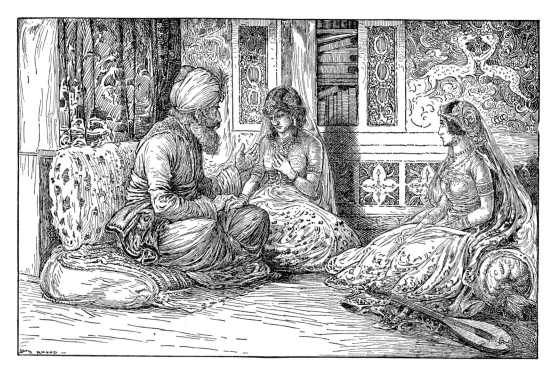

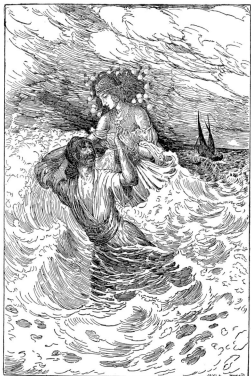
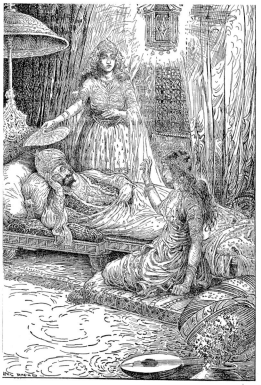

Top: "What happened to the ass?" asked Scheherazade. "I will tell you," said the vizier
Bottom left: I should certainly have perished but for her aid
Bottom right: Scheherazade relating her first story to the Sultan

Louis Rhead, 1916

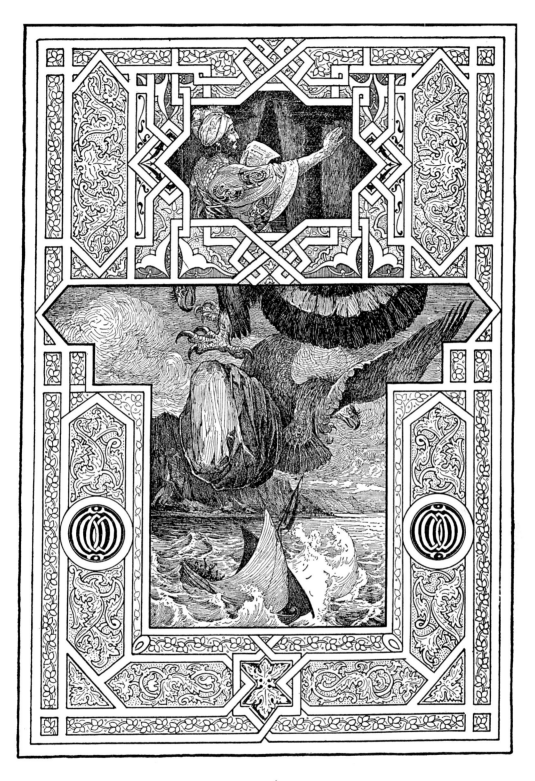

Frontispiece decoration

Louis Rhead, 1916

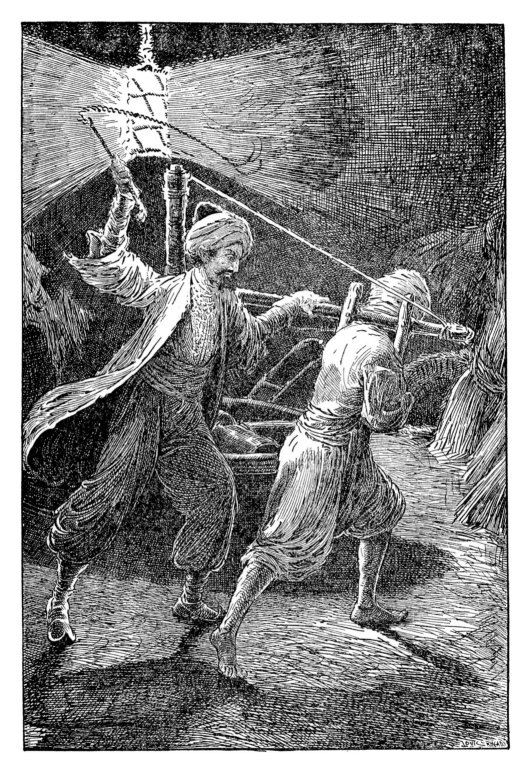

The Miller obliged my brother to turn the mill during the rest of the night

Louis Rhead, 1916

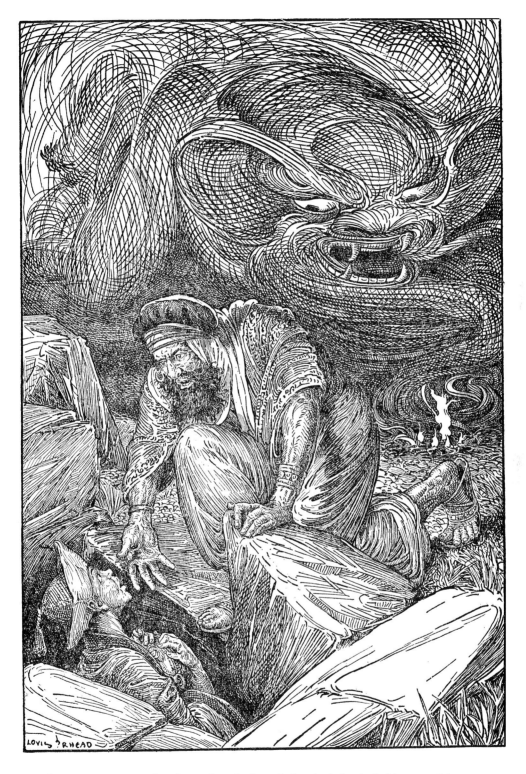

The magician persisted in demanding the lamp before he helped Aladdin out of the cave

Louis Rhead, 1916

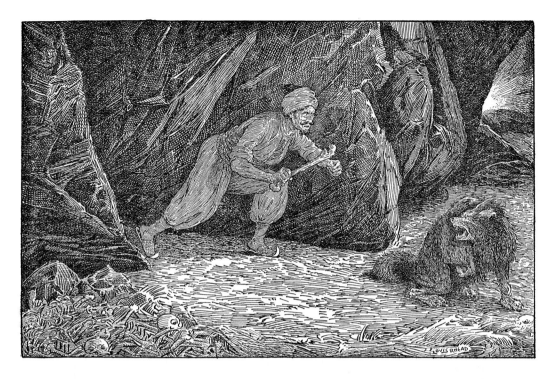

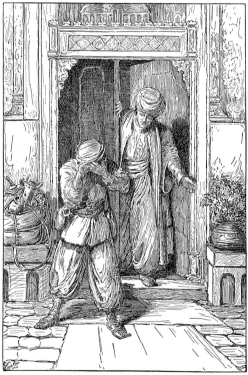

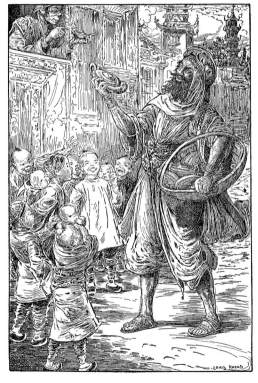

Top: I perceived that the thing which I had heard pant, and which I had followed,
was an animal that lived in the sea

Bottom left: "Come, follow me; my master Sindbad wishes to speak with you"

Bottom right: "Who will exchange old lamps for new ones?"

Louis Rhead, 1916

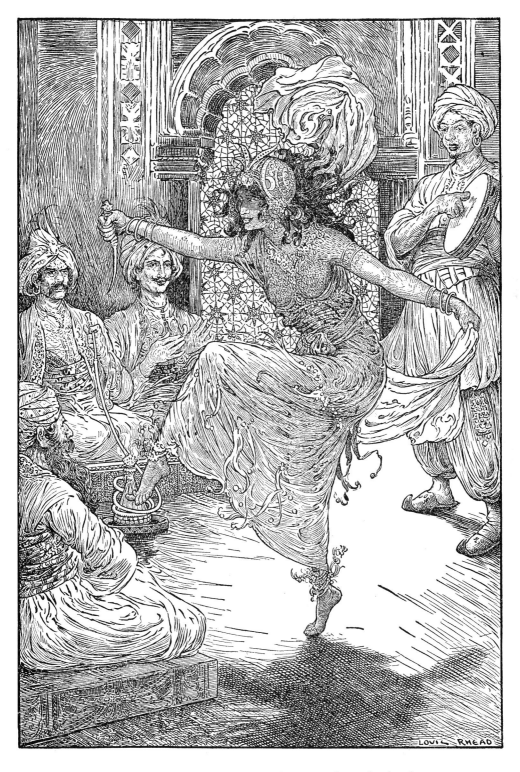

Morgiana drew out the dagger, dancing with it in her hand

Louis Rhead, 1916

Opposite: The Sorceress returned the next day

Charles Robinson, 1913

Charles Robinson
The Story of Prince Ahmed
and the Fairy Perie Banou, 1913

The Robinson family—one of the most successful associations of brothers that the profession of illustration has ever known—had been involved in publishing and illustration for generations. Charles (1870–1937) was the middle of three brothers; Thomas (1865–1950) was his senior, and William (1872–1944) his junior; all three were very active during the Golden Age of Illustration. Charles's big break came in 1895, when he produced over one hundred line drawings for Robert Louis Stevenson's *A Child's Garden of Verses*. The edition was a great success, and it brought Charles new commissions in magazines and books. He became a staple of the gift-book market for the next twenty years, occasionally working with Thomas and William on a single project, though each brother would become successful on his own. Charles Robinson's work on the single tale from the Arabian Nights featured here demonstrates his penchant for working decorative elements into his illustrations.

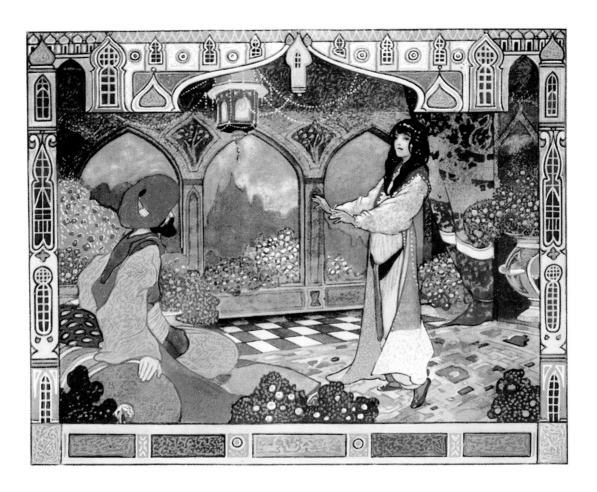

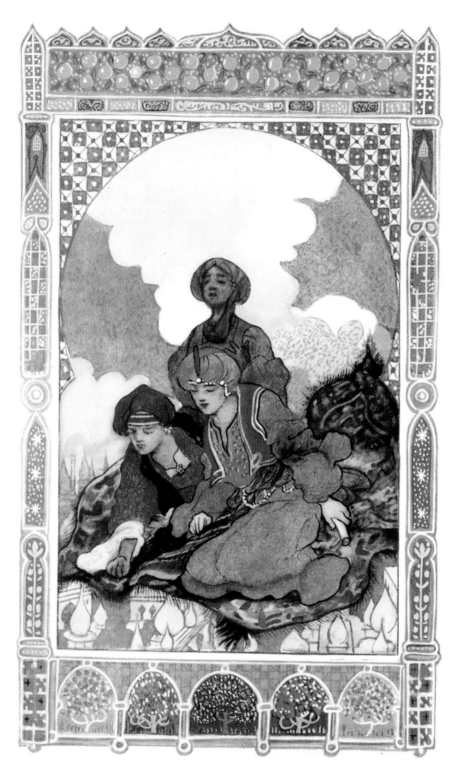

Ali and Ahmed sat down by Houssain and were transported instantaneously

Charles Robinson, 1913

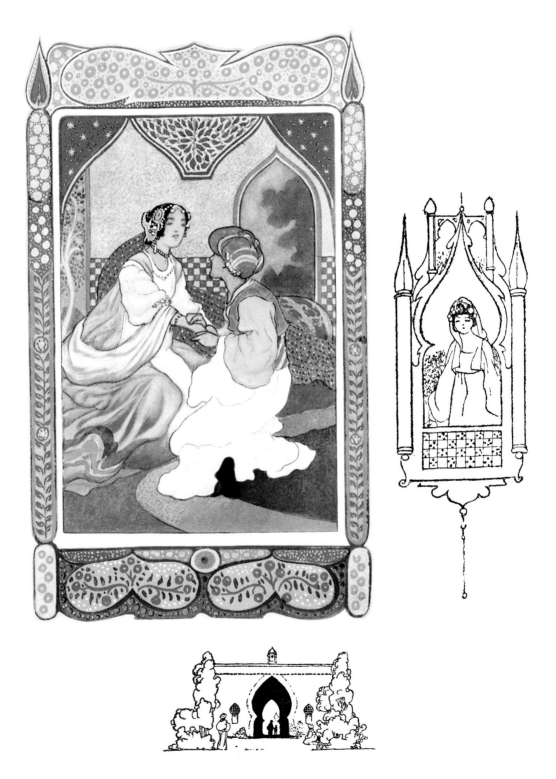

Perie Banou presented her hand

with line decorations

Charles Robinson, 1913

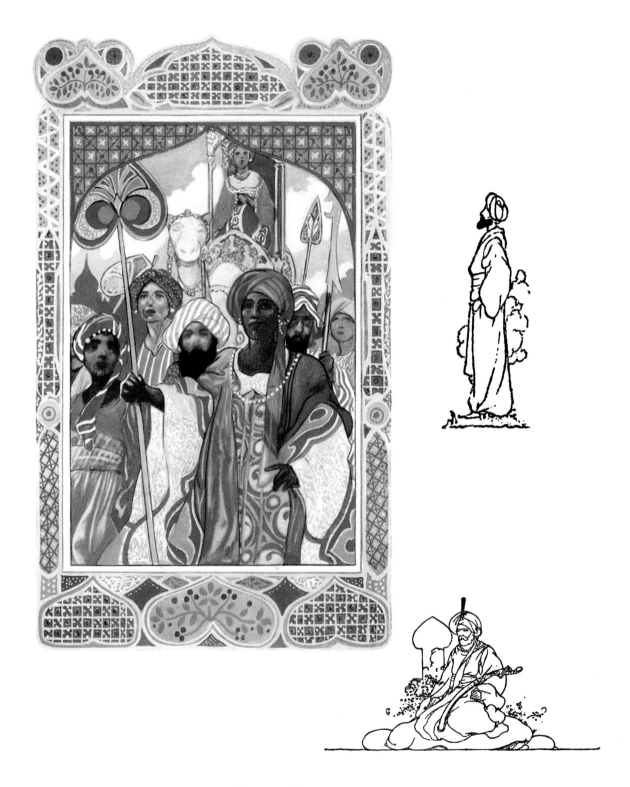

Prince Ahmed took his leave of the fairy

with line decorations

Charles Robinson, 1913

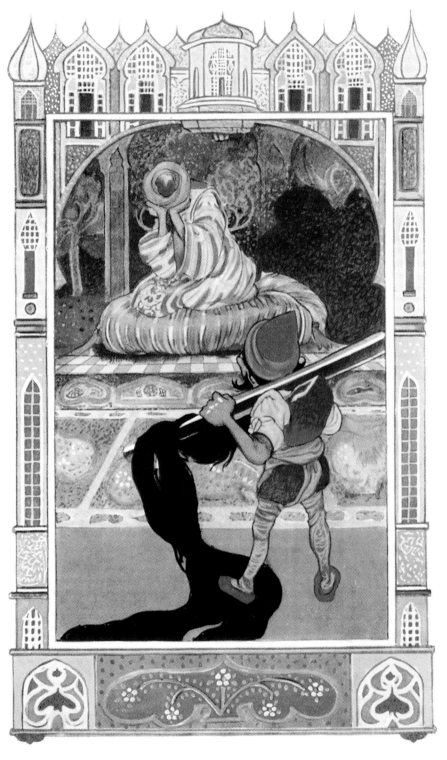

Schaibar, carrying his head erect, went fiercely up to the throne

Charles Robinson, 1913

Opposite: The genie immediately returned with a tray bearing dishes of the most delicious viands

Milo Winter, 1914

Milo Winter
The Arabian Nights Entertainments, 1914

The American illustrator Milo Winter (1888–1956) was born in Illinois; he lived in Chicago and later moved to New York in the early 1950s. Winter illustrated many classic children's book titles in the early twentieth century, such as *Aesop's Fables,* Hans Christian Andersen's fairy tales, *Gulliver's Travels,* and this version of the Arabian Nights. His success with children's books would lead him to work for Childcraft books in 1947 as art editor, and in 1949 he became the art editor of the filmstrip division at Silver-Burdett.

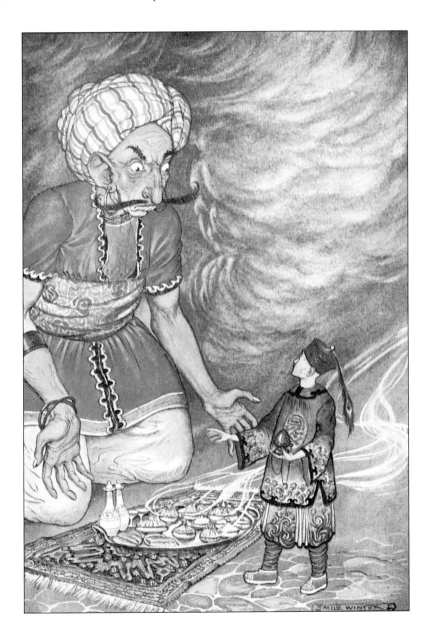

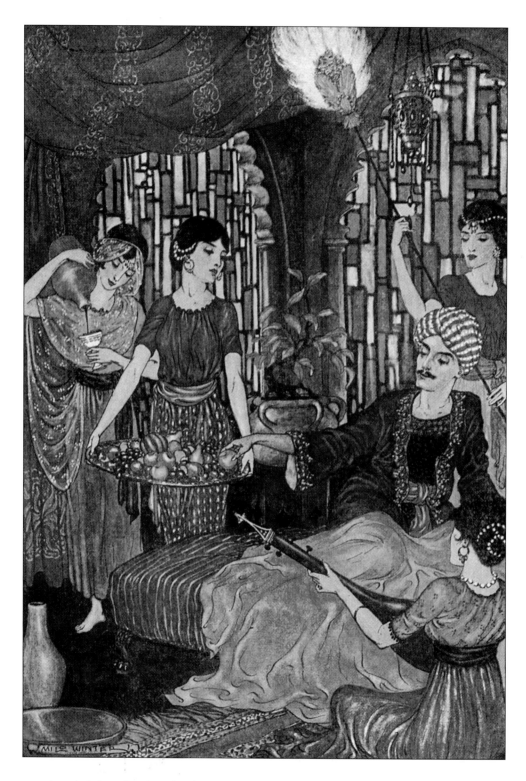

These ladies vied with each other in their eager solicitude to do me all possible service

Milo Winter, 1914

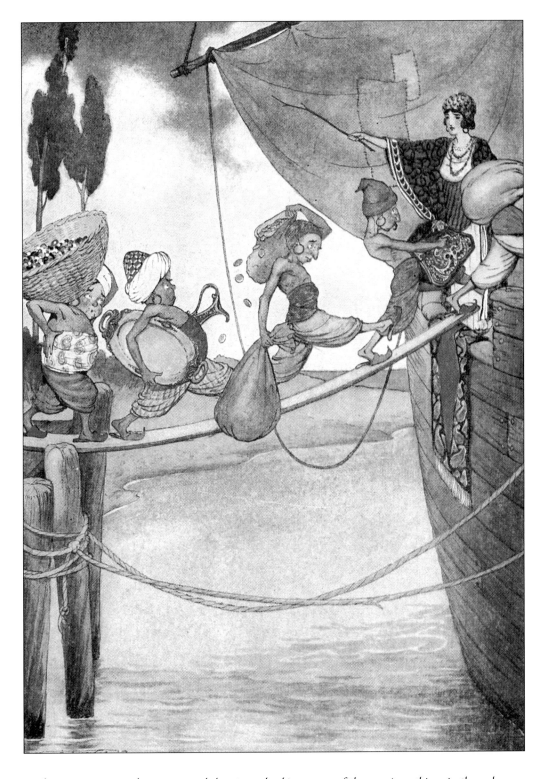

The seamen were taken up several days in embarking many of the precious things in the palace

Milo Winter, 1914

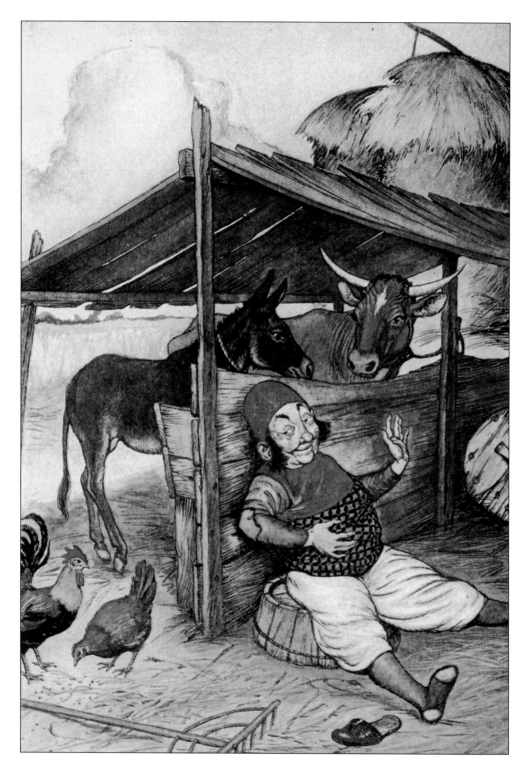

He had the gift of understanding the language of beasts

Milo Winter, 1914

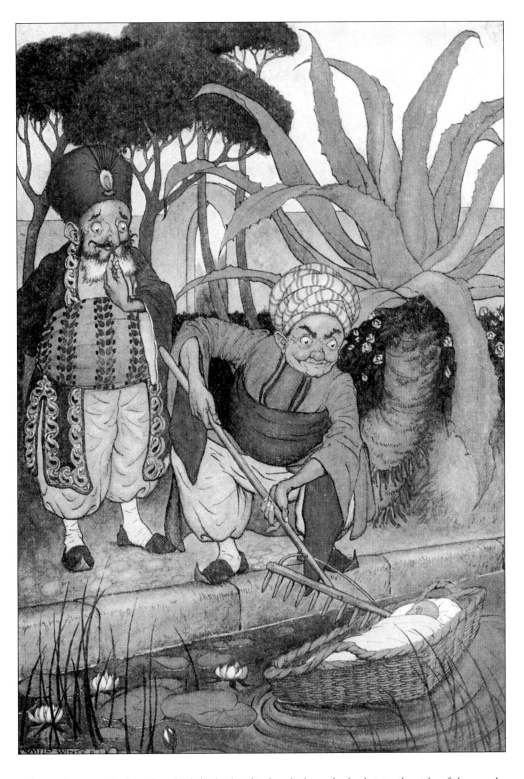

The gardener, with the rake which he had in his hand, drew the basket to the side of the canal

Milo Winter, 1914

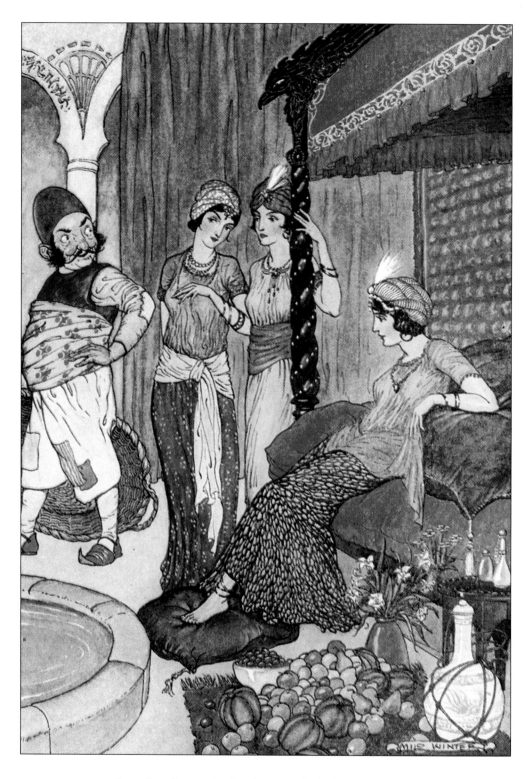

He was chained to the spot by the pleasure of beholding three such beauties

Milo Winter, 1914

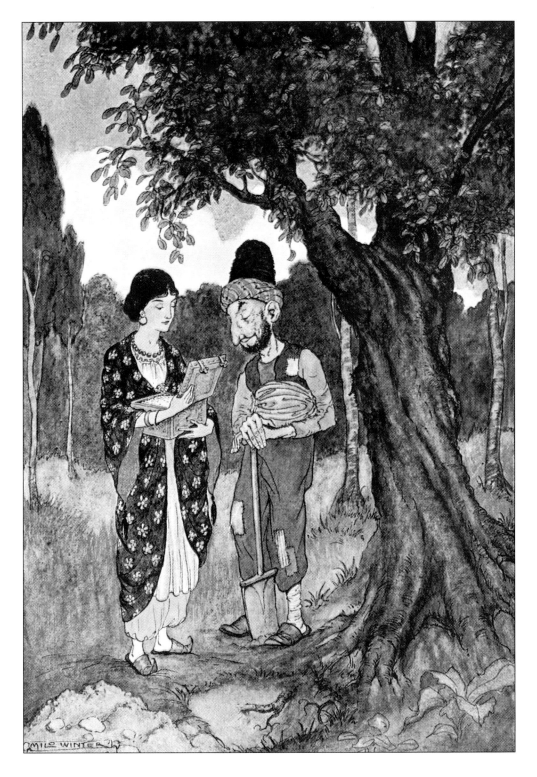

He presently discovered a gold box, about a foot square, which he gave into the princess's hands

Milo Winter, 1914

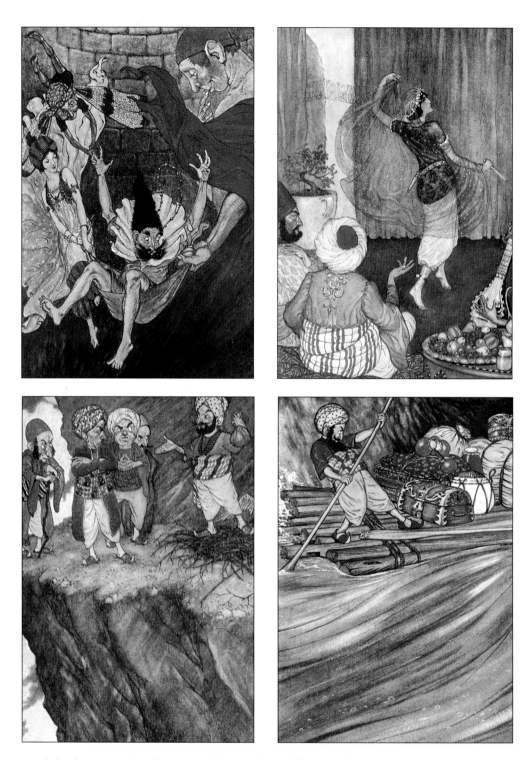

Top left: They received and supported him, and carried him to the bottom, so that he got no hurt

Top right: She drew the poniard, and, holding it in her hand, began a dance

Bottom left: I had scarcely done speaking when the other merchants came crowding about us, much astonished to see me

Bottom right: Having balanced my cargo exactly, and fastened it well to the raft, I went on board with the two oars I had made

Milo Winter, 1914

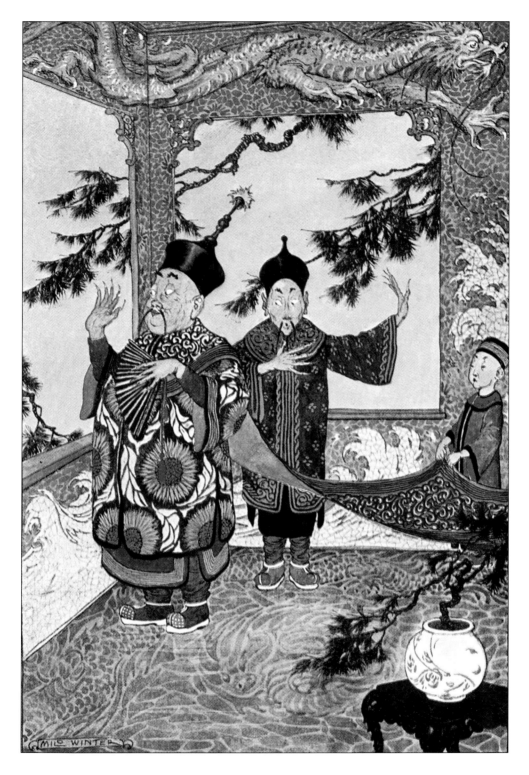

On looking more attentively, he was convinced beyond the power of doubt
that it was his son-in-law's palace

Milo Winter, 1914

THE END

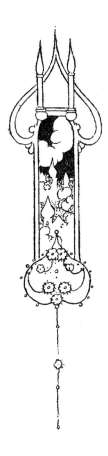